AUNT DIMITY TAKES A HOLIDAY

Nancy Atherton is the author of *Aunt Dimity: Snowbound* and seven other Aunt Dimity novels, all available from Penguin. She lives in Colorado Springs, Colorado.

Aunt Dimity
Takes a Holiday

NANCY ATHERTON

PENGUIN BOOKS

PENGUIN BOOKS

Published by the Penguin Group

Penguin Group (USA) Inc., 375 Hudson Street, New York, New York 10014, U.S.A.

Penguin Books Ltd, 80 Strand, London WC2R 0RL, England

Penguin Books Australia Ltd, 250 Camberwell Road, Camberwell, Victoria 3124, Australia

Penguin Books Canada Ltd, 10 Alcorn Avenue, Toronto, Ontario, Canada M4V 3B2

Penguin Books India (P) Ltd, 11 Community Centre, Panchsheel Park,
New Delhi – 110 017, India

Penguin Books (N.Z.) Ltd, Cnr Rosedale and Airborne Roads, Albany, Auckland,
New Zealand

Penguin Books (South Africa) (Pty) Ltd, 24 Sturdee Avenue, Rosebank, Johannesburg
2196, South Africa

Penguin Books Ltd, Registered Offices: 80 Strand, London WC2R 0RL, England

First published in the United States of America by Viking Penguin,
a member of Penguin Group (USA) Inc. 2003
Published in Penguin Books 2004

10 9 8 7 6 5

THE LIBRARY OF CONGRESS HAS CATALOGUED
THE HARDCOVER EDITION AS FOLLOWS:
Atherton, Nancy.
Aunt Dimity takes a holiday / Nancy Atherton.
p. cm.
ISBN 0-670-03200-X (hc.)
ISBN 0 14 20.0393 X (pbk.)
1. Dimity, Aunt (Fictitious character)—Fiction.   2. Women detectives—England—
Cotswold Hills—Fiction.   3. Cotswold Hills (England)—Fiction.   I. Title.
PS3551.T426 A9345 2003
813'.54—dc21   2002028095

Printed in the United States of America

For Elizabeth Slusser,
who listened,
and
Christine Aden,
who answered the call

Aunt Dimity
Takes a Holiday

One

$\mathcal{I}$t was supposed to be a quiet afternoon.

Bill and I had spent the morning imbibing vast quantities of fresh air while endeavoring to keep our three-year-old twins from becoming too closely acquainted with all creatures, great and small, at the Cotswolds Farm Park. It had been no easy task. Will and Rob had made heroic efforts to pet each and every one of the park's polka-dotted sheep, crested hens, and striped pigs, and it had taken brute force to prevent them from climbing into the pens to shake hooves with the gentle but gigantic Shire horses.

My husband had chosen to recuperate from his exertions by joining the boys in an afternoon nap, but I'd opted for a cup of tea before the fire in the living room. Quiet moments had become as rare as polka-dotted sheep since the twins had learned to trot and I wanted to savor the tranquillity while it lasted.

It lasted for precisely seven minutes.

The mantel clock was chiming the hour when a thunderous knocking sounded at my front door. I jumped, splashed my hand with scalding tea, and vowed to throttle the nitwit whose thoughtless pounding threatened to rouse my slumbering menfolk. Infuriated, indignant, and in pain, I charged into the hallway, flung the front door wide, and froze.

My friend and neighbor Emma Harris stood on the doorstep, but it was not the Emma Harris I knew. *My* Emma wasn't given to displays of strong emotion, but the Emma standing on my doorstep looked angry enough to chew barbed wire.

"Lori, let me in or there'll be *bloodshed*."

I looked down at her clenched fists, decided to avoid the shedding of my own personal blood, and stepped aside.

As Emma stormed past me and into the living room, I glanced outside, saw neither horse nor car, and concluded that she'd walked the mile-long path that wound from her fourteenth-century manor house to my cottage. Emma usually savored woodland walks, but something told me that today's outing had been more of a quick march than a pleasant stroll.

I closed the door, crept cautiously back to the living room, and sank onto the sofa in cowed silence while Emma paced back and forth before the fire, caught up in what appeared to be deeply unpleasant thoughts.

Emma had shed some forty pounds of excess weight over the past year and cut her flowing gray-blond hair to shoulder length. The woman who had once resembled a cuddly koala now moved with the contained ferocity of a caged lioness. When she came to an abrupt halt before me, I had to restrain the urge to shrink back out of reach of her claws.

"What," she demanded, "is your husband's name?"

"Bill," I replied obediently, adding for good measure, "Bill Willis. William Arthur Willis, Junior, to be precise."

"Are you sure?" she snapped. "The only reason I ask is that, until this morning, I thought I knew *my* husband's name."

I blinked. "It's not Derek Harris?"

"Ha." Emma glared at me through her wire-rimmed glasses. "The husband formerly known as Derek Harris is, in fact, Anthony Evelyn Armstrong Seton, Viscount Hailesham."

Emma gave the title the correct upper-crust English pronunciation, which involved swallowing half the vowels and producing something that sounded vaguely like a sneeze: "*Hell*-shm."

"Your husband is Viscount Hailesham," I said somberly. "Of course he is. And I am Marie of Romania."

Emma's gray eyes flashed. "This is no time for your silly jokes, Lori."

"Then it must be time for a sedative because you're talking *crazy,* Emma." I got to my feet and met her glare with a potent one of my own. "Now sit down, calm down, and explain to me why your husband of ten years, a man who respects, admires, and loves you beyond reason, would bother to lie to you about his identity."

"Because," she came back crisply, "he *hates* his *father.*"

Emma turned on her heel and stalked over to sit in my favorite armchair, leaving me to connect the dots while she seethed.

My glare faded to a thoughtful glimmer as I resumed my seat. Derek Harris had never said much to me about his background. I had the faint notion that his father was an earl and that the two had been estranged for many years, but beyond that I knew very little.

"Do you know where he got the name Derek Harris?"

Emma asked, then rushed on without waiting for a reply. "From a carpenter on the family estate. My husband the viscount became Mr. Derek Harris as an act of defiance after his father threatened to disinherit him."

"Why did his father threaten to disinherit him?" I asked.

"Because Derek wanted to work with his hands," Emma replied. "The ninth Earl Elstyn couldn't bear the thought of his son and heir becoming a manual laborer."

"A manual laborer?" My eyebrows rose. Emma's husband was a contractor who specialized in the restoration of historic buildings. He was one of the most highly respected authorities in his field. No one but the most narrow-minded of snobs would dismiss him as a mere manual laborer. "Does the earl have a clear idea of what Derek does for a living?"

"How would I know?" said Emma. "The two haven't spoken in twenty years. That's when Derek defied his father a second time by marrying Mary." She tossed her head in disdain. "Evidently Mary's blood wasn't blue enough to suit Lord Elstyn."

I curled my legs beneath me, intrigued by the unfolding family saga. I was familiar with the tragic story of Mary, Derek's first wife, who'd died shortly after giving birth to their second child. Derek had once told me that it had taken years for him to recover from the loss, and a minor miracle for him to find Emma and fall in love all over again.

"If Lord Elstyn disapproved of Mary, God knows what he'll make of me," Emma said fretfully. "At least she was English. I'm not only a commoner, I'm an *American*."

"Which means that he defied his father yet again when he married you," I pointed out. "What does Derek's mother think?"

"Derek's mother died when he was a child," Emma replied. "His father never remarried. He must have figured he'd produced an heir, so why bother going through *that* again?"

I rubbed my nose, bemused. "I have to confess that I never thought of Derek as a rebel."

"I never thought of him as a viscount," Emma grumbled.

"What about the children?" I asked. "Peter and Nell have always gotten along with their grandfather, haven't they? They stay with him often enough." Sixteen-year-old Nell had, in fact, spent most of the past summer at Lord Elstyn's estate. "Why would Derek allow them to visit a father he hates?"

"That's Mary's doing." Emma's stormy expression softened. "As she lay dying, Mary made Derek promise to keep their children out of his quarrel with his father. Derek couldn't go back on a deathbed promise, so Peter and Nell have always been allowed to spend as much time with their grandfather as they wished."

"I don't understand why the earl would want to spend time with Peter and Nell," I said. "He rejected Mary as a commoner. What's kept him from rejecting her children?"

"He doesn't have much choice," Emma explained. "Peter and Nell are his only legitimate grandchildren. It's either accept them or leave Hailesham to some distant cousin."

"Hailesham?" My jaw dropped. "As in Hailesham Park? The place in Wiltshire you told me about? The place with the amazing gardens?"

Emma's eyes narrowed dangerously. "I've avoided those gardens for years, for Derek's sake, but now that I know they belong to *him*—"

"Hailesham Park belongs to *Derek?*" I squeaked.

"Not yet," said Emma, "but it will when he inherits the title."

"Which title?" I said breathlessly.

"You haven't been paying attention, Lori," Emma scolded. "Derek isn't simply Lord Elstyn's oldest son, he's Lord Elstyn's *only* son—his *only child*. When the earl dies, Derek will inherit *everything*."

"How?" I wrinkled my nose in confusion. "I'd have thought—"

"Me, too," Emma interrupted. "But apparently no one minds if you change your name, loathe your father, and abandon your family for twenty years, so long as you don't relinquish your titles."

"Which Derek hasn't done," I ventured, and when Emma bridled impatiently, I hurried on. "Okay. Let me get this straight." I leaned forward, elbows on knees, and concentrated. "Derek is Viscount Hailesham, his father is the ninth Earl Elstyn, and the family seat is Hailesham Park, which Derek will inherit when his father dies." I gazed at Emma in wonderment. "And this somehow escaped your attention until this morning?"

"Derek's always been tight-lipped about his family, and I respected his right to keep that part of his life separate from ours," Emma said. "I knew his father was an earl, but I didn't think it *meant* anything. I didn't think it had anything to do with *me*. But it does." She gulped. "Derek explained the situation to me this morning because he had to, Lori. We've been summoned to Hailesham Park."

I nearly laughed. "How can Lord Elstyn summon a son he hasn't spoken to in twenty years?"

"By making Nell his messenger," Emma answered.

I smiled wryly. "Derek's never been able to say no to Lady Nell."

"Nell's not a lady," Emma informed me. "She's only an honorable until Derek inherits his father's title."

"An honorable?" I felt as if I were being pummeled with a copy of *Debrett's Peerage*. "Sorry, Emma, you're losing me again."

"I know how you feel." She breathed a wistful sigh. "Yesterday I was plain old Mrs. Derek Harris. Today I'm the Right Honorable the Viscountess Hailesham. Lori," she said, *"I don't know how to be a viscountess!"*

It wasn't until I heard the desperation in Emma's voice that I finally understood why she was behaving so strangely. She wasn't angry. She was terrified. I wondered if I'd feel the same way if I awoke one day to find myself married to an English peer, but since Bill and I were both Americans, I doubted I'd ever get the chance to find out.

"Just, er, be yourself," I offered.

"Be myself?" Emma exclaimed. "I'm a gardener, Lori. If I were myself, I'd spend the next ten days manuring my roses. Instead I have to spend them getting ready to face a hostile tribe of aristocrats on their home turf. It's a family reunion, for heaven's sake. It's supposed to last five days. I don't know what to wear or what to say or how to act." She buried her face in her hands. "I just know I'm going to make a fool of myself."

A surge of envy made me less sympathetic to her plight than I might otherwise have been.

"You get to spend five days at Hailesham?" I sighed rapturously. "I'd give my eyeteeth to spend five days in that house."

Emma raised her head. "Hand them over, then," she said, "because I want you to come with me."

I could scarcely believe my ears. "Don't toy with me, Emma."

"I'm not toying with you. I need moral support. Besides," she added pensively, "I may need your help to prevent a murder."

Two

efore I could give Emma's stunning postscript the response it deserved, I heard the sound of Bill's footsteps on the staircase. Emma must have heard it, too, because she sprang to my side.

"Don't mention the murder," she whispered urgently.

"B-but—" I stammered.

"Hi, Bill," Emma said, straightening.

"Hello, Emma. Forgive my dishabille. I've been napping." My husband entered the living room looking refreshed and comfortably rumpled in a pair of black jeans and a forest-green sweater. He leaned over the back of the sofa to kiss the nape of my neck. "Why didn't you tell me we had company?"

I was still staring, round-eyed, at Emma, so she took it upon herself to answer Bill.

"We didn't want to disturb your beauty sleep," she teased. "Nell sends her best, by the way. I wasn't sure about her going to the Sorbonne, but she seems to be flourishing. . . ."

While Emma rambled on about her stepdaughter, I continued to gape at her, nonplussed. Who was about to be murdered? How had she gotten wind of the impending crime? Why was she asking for my help instead of calling in the police? What, exactly, did she expect me to do? My brain was churning with so many questions that I nearly missed Bill's departure.

"Good Lord, is that the time?" he said, glancing at his watch. "Sorry, Emma, I have to run. Annelise is coming back from Altnaharra today and I promised to pick her up at the train station."

Annelise Sciaparrelli, our saintly nanny, had spent the past month visiting her sister and archaeologist brother-in-law at a dig in the Scottish hinterlands. As much as Bill and I had enjoyed our time alone with our sons, we were—all four of us—looking forward to Annelise's return.

Bill paused on his way out to peer down at me. "Are you all right, Lori? You seem . . . dazed."

"Do I?" I forced a cheery smile. "Still drunk on fresh air, I guess. I probably should have taken a nap."

"We can both catch up on our sleep, now that Annelise is coming home." He ruffled my short crop of dark curls, said good-bye to Emma, and headed for the hallway.

Emma said nothing until Bill had closed the front door behind him.

"Now, Lori," she began, "don't get overexcited."

I wanted to shake her. "You can't drop the word *murder* into a conversation, then tell me not to get overexcited," I sputtered. "What murder? Whose?"

"Derek's." Emma held her hands up for silence and flopped down next to me on the sofa. "I know I sound like a hysterical wife, but think about it, Lori. Derek's the black sheep of his family. He's also next in line to inherit his father's fortune. What if someone thinks the black sheep doesn't deserve his inheritance?" Emma looked anxiously toward the bay window. "I have a terrible feeling that someone might try to prune a branch from the family tree."

Emma Harris was not a flighty woman. Compared to me, she was as grounded as an ancient oak. If she felt uneasy about Derek's safety, it wasn't because she had an overactive imagination.

I sat back, folded my arms, and tried to view the situation from her perspective.

"Family reunions can be tricky," I observed sagely. "You never know when old resentments will rear their ugly heads. And I suppose a powerful family might store up some pretty powerful resentments."

Emma's shoulder touched mine as she settled back against the cushions.

"Normal people fall out over who gets Aunt Mildred's crocheted tablecloth," she commented. "In this case we're talking about Aunt Mildred's priceless collection of Rembrandts."

I gave her a sidelong look. "Is Derek's family really that rich?"

"Lord Elstyn frequently takes Nell to lunch," Emma replied, "on his *yacht*. In *Monte Carlo*."

"Ah."

We gazed thoughtfully into the fire.

"Five days in an isolated location," I murmured. "Five days surrounded by potentially hostile cousins. Who knows what might happen?"

"You know how obsessive Derek is about fixing things," Emma said morosely. "Someone will point out a loose shingle, Derek will climb up to nail it in place, and, whoops, there goes the ladder." She turned to me. "If you come with me, we'll be able to keep an eye on him *at all times.*"

"Does Derek know you're worried about him?" I asked.

"He thinks I'm being melodramatic," said Emma. "And paranoid. And basically silly. That's why I don't want you to mention it to Bill. I don't want the two of them to start poking fun at me."

"Have you talked it over with Nicholas?" Nicholas Fox was a police detective on medical leave who was staying at the Harrises' manor house.

"Nicholas needs peace and quiet," said Emma, shaking her head. "I don't want him fretting about Derek."

"What about Kit?" I suggested. "He won't accuse you of being silly."

Kit Smith lived at Anscombe Manor, too, in a private flat overlooking the stable yard. He was the Harrises' stable master, one of my dearest friends, and the single most selfless soul I'd ever met. If anyone would help Emma in her hour of need, it would be Kit.

"I haven't spoken with Kit," Emma said carefully. "He might volunteer to accompany us to Hailesham and I don't think that would be a good idea. Do you?"

"Not if Nell's there," I said.

"Nell will be there," Emma said quietly. "She's flying in from Paris to attend the family meeting."

Emma didn't need to explain further. I was fully aware of the trouble Nell Harris had caused when she'd bombarded Kit Smith with love letters the previous winter. The poor man had done everything he could to discourage her amorous attentions, pointing out that he was twice her age and therefore quite unsuitable, but Nell had pursued him relentlessly. We'd been relieved when she'd gone off to spend the summer with her grandfather, and delighted by her unexpected decision to spend a year at the Sorbonne.

Kit hadn't heard from Nell since she'd left. I hoped that absence had failed to make Nell's heart grow fonder, but I also agreed with Emma: It would be tempting fate to take Kit to Hailesham Park while Nell was there.

"Well," I said, "I guess that leaves me."

Emma peered at me hopefully. "You'll come?"

"I haven't left the cottage since we got back from the States in April. I could do with a holiday." I nodded decisively. "Count me in."

"Thanks so much, Lori. Maybe I am being silly, but if not . . ." Emma smiled briefly, but there was a worried frown behind the smile. "I may not want to be a viscountess, but I don't want to be a widow even more."

Derek a rebel, Lady Nell a lowly honorable, and Emma a viscountess—I thought the surprises were over for the day, but Bill had saved a final one for after dinner.

The dishes had been washed, the boys had been put to bed, and Annelise had retired early to her room to recover from train lag. Bill and I were alone at last, entwined upon the sofa, bathed in the fire's rosy glow, contented, serene, and almost ready to crawl upstairs to bed. The time seemed ripe to broach the subject of my trip to Hailesham Park.

Since Emma had asked me to keep her fears to myself,

I focused instead on her need for moral support and my own excitement at the prospect of roving unhindered through the private precincts of Lord Elstyn's grand estate. When I'd finished spinning my tale, Bill favored me with a quizzical smile.

"You can go with Derek and Emma if you like," he said, "but I'd rather you come with me."

"Where are you going?" I asked.

"To Hailesham," he replied.

I lifted my head from his chest and peered up at him. "Since when are you going to Hailesham?"

"I planned to tell you about it this evening," Bill explained. "Lord Elstyn has invited us both to Hailesham, to attend the family meeting."

"Why would he invite us?" I said, taken aback.

My husband's velvety brown eyes grew suspiciously round and innocent. "Didn't I say? I'm one of Lord Elstyn's attorneys. He wants me to be on hand while he takes care of some family business. It'll be a working holiday for me, but I thought you might like to come along."

"You thought . . ." I unentwined myself from Bill and slid to the far end of the sofa. "How long have you been Lord Elstyn's attorney?"

Bill cleared his throat and carefully avoided my eyes. "The earl's involvement in various financial concerns in the United States made it advisable for him to retain me as his legal counsel approximately three months ago."

"You're talking like a lawyer, Bill."

"I am a lawyer, Lori."

We stared at each other across a sofa that seemed to lengthen by the minute. My husband was, in fact, the head of the European branch of Willis & Willis, his family's venerable law firm. I should have been proud of him for nabbing such a prestigious client. Instead I felt a prickle of resentment.

"You've known about Derek for three months and never breathed a word to me?" I said.

"I couldn't," said Bill. "Lord Elstyn's business requires complete confidentiality."

I eyed him reproachfully but gave a reluctant nod of understanding. My husband was paid big bucks to keep his mouth shut. It was unfair of me to expect him to divulge his clients' secrets, even when they concerned our closest friends in England.

"I've never been to Hailesham Park," Bill said by way of a peace offering. "I've never set foot in Hailesham House."

I looked at him, puzzled. "Then where . . . ?"

"The London office," said Bill. "And I've only met Lord Elstyn in person twice. He prefers to work through intermediaries."

Mollified, I asked, "Does he look like Derek?"

"Come with me to Hailesham and find out." Bill opened his arms.

"Oh, Bill, of course I'm coming with you." Sighing deeply, I slid over and curled close to him again. "But I have to tell you: There are times when I absolutely *hate* attorney-client privilege."

Bill wrapped his arms around me. "Sometimes I hate it, too, love."

I rested my head upon his chest and gazed into the glowing embers. However glad I was that the evening's conversation had ended amicably, I was gladder still that

I'd kept my promise to Emma. Our loving husbands had been keeping one too many secrets from us lately. It seemed only fair that we keep a few from them.

Besides, I didn't need Bill's help to protect Derek. As a mother of twin boys I'd developed a preternatural awareness of danger. I could spot a broken bottle at forty paces. I could smell a smoldering cigarette butt a mile away. I'd stared down growling dogs, hissing geese, and closet monsters. I was more than capable of handling whatever the Elstyn clan might throw at Derek.

It wasn't the danger that unnerved me so much as the dress code. Unlike Bill, who'd been born with silver spoons spilling out of his mouth, I wasn't used to hobnobbing with the gentry. As I lay cuddled against my husband, I began to wonder if Emma had invited me along as a guarantee that she wouldn't be alone in making a fool of herself.

Would we be expected to dress for dinner? I wondered. If so, what kind of dress would be appropriate? I was in no mood to ask Bill for advice, but I knew someone else I could turn to. I waited until Bill's steady breathing told me he'd fallen asleep, then disengaged myself from his arms and headed for the study.

Three

$\mathcal{I}$ hadn't always lived a life of leisure in the English countryside. While my husband had grown up in a mansion filled with servants, I'd been raised by my widowed mother in a modest apartment building in a working-class Chicago neighborhood.

We weren't poor because my mother worked long and hard to keep our heads above water. There must have been days when she wanted to chuck her job and run away with the circus, but she never did. Her devotion to me enabled her to stay the course, as did her friendship with an Englishwoman named Dimity Westwood.

My mother and Dimity met in London while serving their respective countries during the Second World War. The two women became fast friends while the blitz was raging, and they wrote letters to each other for the rest of their lives. Their transatlantic correspondence was a refuge to which my mother could retreat when the world around her became too dreary or too burdensome to bear.

My mother was very protective of her refuge. Instead of telling me about her friend directly, she introduced me to her obliquely, as a character in a series of bedtime stories. The redoubtable Aunt Dimity was as familiar to me as Sleeping Beauty was to other children, but I knew nothing of Dimity Westwood until after both she and my mother had died.

It was then that the real-life Dimity became my benefactress, bequeathing to me a comfortable fortune, a honey-colored cottage in the Cotswolds, and a journal bound in dark blue leather. The money was a lifesaver and the cottage a dream come true, but the journal was Dimity's greatest gift to me, for in it she'd left something of herself.

Literally.

Whenever I opened the blue journal, its blank pages came alive with Dimity's handwriting, a graceful copperplate taught in the village school at a time when horse-drawn plows outnumbered tractors. I'd been scared spitless the first time Dimity had greeted me from beyond the grave, but fear had long since given way to gratitude. I simply couldn't imagine life without my good and trusted, if not entirely corporeal, friend.

I closed the study door, turned on the mantelpiece lamps, took the blue journal from its niche on the bookshelves, and curled comfortably in one of the pair of leather armchairs that sat before the hearth.

"Dimity?" I said, opening the journal. "Got a minute?" I glanced briefly at the door, then smiled down at the journal as Dimity's words began to unfurl across the page.

I have several, as it happens, each of which is at your disposal.

"Great," I said, "because I've got the most astonishing news to tell you. Derek Harris is a *viscount*."

Ah. There was a pause before Dimity added, *Is that the astonishing news?*

"Well . . . yes," I said, deflated. I'd expected at least one or two exclamation points.

I'm sorry, my dear, but I can't pretend to be too terribly aston-ished. I've been acquainted with Derek's father for many years, you see. I'm well aware of Derek's position among the Elstyns.

I suppressed a soft groan of frustration. "Am I the only person in the cottage who *didn't* know that Derek was a big-shot aristocrat?"

I doubt that Will and Rob are aware of Derek's title.

"I wouldn't be so sure," I said. "Bill probably confided in them three months ago. That's when he became Lord Elstyn's lawyer."

How interesting. Edwin's American investments must be doing well if he requires the services of Willis & Willis.

"Edwin?" I said, blinking. "You were on a first-name ba-sis with Lord Elstyn?"

Indeed I was. Edwin made several generous donations to the Westwood Trust. If you look in the archives, you'll find his name on many donors' lists.

The Westwood Trust was an umbrella organization for a number of charities that had been close to Dimity's heart. As its titular head, I sat in on board meetings and planning sessions, but it had never occurred to me to go rooting around in its archives.

"Lord Elstyn may have been generous to the trust," I al-lowed, "but his idea of charity isn't the kind that begins at home. Emma told me he's been pretty hard on Derek."

The two men have always been hard on each other. Edwin was furious with Derek for rejecting a career in politics or finance, and Derek was furious with Edwin for disparaging his passion for restoration work. Both were too stiff-necked to attempt a compro-mise, and the result was an unfortunate estrangement.

"What about Derek's first wife?" I asked. "Lord Elstyn looked down his nose at her, didn't he?"

If one's son is to inherit a vast and complex family fortune, one naturally wishes for a suitable daughter-in-law. Edwin considered Mary to be most unsuitable.

I bristled. "Because she was a commoner, like me?"

Mary wasn't remotely like you, Lori. She was sweet and helpless and altogether incapable of running such a demanding household. Edwin was not entirely wrong to assume that she would have been lost as mistress of Hailesham Park.

I was a bit put out by Dimity's suggestion that I lacked sweetness but had to agree with her about running a place like Hailesham. I found it challenging enough to keep the cottage neat and tidy. It would be a thousand times more difficult to manage a large estate.

"Maybe Derek chose his wife with his heart instead of his head," I said. "It may not have been the practical thing to do, but since when does love have anything to do with practicality?"

Love has, alas, always been less important to Edwin than duty. He married for practical reasons and could not understand his son's refusal to do as he had done.

"It sounds as if Derek hasn't done anything his father wanted him to do," I commented. "Until now, that is. Emma came over today to tell me that Derek's accepted the earl's invitation to attend a family reunion at Hailesham Park. Derek's going home for the first time in twenty years, and he's taking Emma with him. How's that for astonishing?"

Nothing could be more predictable. Derek's approaching his midforties, Lori. One's perceptions change when one reaches middle age, especially when one has a son of one's own. Will Peter be at Hailesham?

"I don't think so." Last I'd heard, Derek's twenty-year-old son was studying whales off the coast of New Zealand. "He's on a research ship somewhere in the South Pacific. I doubt that he'll be able to get back in time to attend the earl's powwow."

His absence may explain Derek's decision to return home. Peter will one day inherit Hailesham Park—and all that comes with it—from his father. Derek might willingly forgo his own inheritance, but he won't jeopardize Peter's. It seems likely that Derek is returning to Hailesham in order to protect his son's claims.

"Do you think someone might challenge him?" I asked.

It's possible. Derek has exiled himself from his family for the past twenty years. There may be those who question his right to don his father's mantle after such a lengthy and self-imposed absence.

I leaned closer to the journal and said, in a confidential murmur, "Do you think there might be . . . violence?"

What a perfectly preposterous suggestion. Honestly, Lori, you must learn to control your penchant for melodrama.

"It wasn't my idea," I protested. "It's Emma's. She's afraid someone might try to murder Derek."

Emma is clearly having trouble adjusting to her new role as viscountess. Please remind her that we are no longer living in the fifteenth century. Poison-filled rings have gone out of style, even in the most aristocratic circles.

I sat back, feeling vaguely disappointed. I'd rather enjoyed the air of intrigue Emma's suspicions had lent the trip.

"Someone might try to fake an accident," I suggested.

And someone might challenge Derek to a duel at dawn, but I think it highly unlikely, don't you?

I was beginning to understand why Emma had been reluctant to broadcast her concerns to the men. Dimity's mild sarcasm was bad enough. Our husbands' combined mockery would have been unbearable.

"I suppose you're right," I mumbled, and moved on to another subject. "Bill and I are going to Hailesham, too. Bill's going as Lord Elstyn's lawyer and I'm tagging along as the lawyer's wife." I hesitated. "I was kind of hoping you'd join us."

I'd be delighted. I haven't visited Hailesham Park in donkey's years. I could do with a holiday.

"It'll be a working holiday," I warned. "I'll need your advice on which fork to use and when to curtsy and what to wear to dinner."

Curtsies are reserved for the Royal Family nowadays, but I'll be more than happy to draw labeled diagrams of typical place settings. As to what to wear . . . Oh, this shall be fun!

Emma had expended too much shocked indignation on her own husband to have much left for mine. When I told her that Bill had been secretly employed by her father-in-law for the past three months, she sighed wearily and said, "I'm tired of boys' games. Let's go shopping." We spent the next week buying clothes.

Emma hadn't replenished her wardrobe since she'd dumped her excess poundage, so our shopping spree was more enjoyable than either of us expected it to be. We purchased riding outfits and hiking gear, were measured for tea gowns and dinner dresses, and selected—at Dimity's insistence—the sort of nightclothes that could be worn while searching chilly corridors for distant bathrooms.

Then came the hunt for shoes to go with each outfit, bags to go with the shoes, and a few simple pieces of jewelry to add sparkle to our ensemble. When Bill asked about our extended shopping trips, I explained to him what Dimity had explained to me: Five days in a country house was equivalent to six months in a foreign country. One had to be prepared for anything.

I made no attempt to tame my unruly curls, knowing that they'd refuse to cooperate in any case, but Emma had her gray-blond hair styled in a becoming bob. The new haircut seemed to bolster her self-confidence. By the time we left the salon, she'd stopped scolding me for addressing her as Viscountess.

As I surveyed my new finery, I took particular pleasure in a slinky black number I'd found at Nanny Cole's Boutique in London. It fit me like a glove and would, I knew, knock Bill's eyes right out of their sockets. When I thought of what else it would do to him, I realized that it was an extremely selfish purchase.

I hadn't felt like such a girly-girl in years and I reveled in every giddy minute. It took me half a day to pack my new clothes—in tissue paper, as Dimity suggested—and I finished by tucking Reginald into my shoulder bag. Reginald was a small, powder-pink stuffed rabbit who'd been with me since childhood, and a powder-pink rabbit was, in my opinion, the perfect complement to a girly-girl's wardrobe.

For the first time since I'd known her, I was glad that Dimity was less than three-dimensional. If we'd had to cart her holiday frocks to Hailesham Park along with mine, we'd have needed a moving truck. As it was, I had to endure endless ribbing from Bill—"Have you packed my spare truss, dear?"——as we loaded my suitcases into his silver-gray Mercedes. The teasing made me more determined than ever to handle my bodyguarding duties without his help.

Dimity might scoff till her ink turned purple, but a promise was a promise. Although I agreed with her that poisoned rings and dueling pistols were no longer in fashion, I also agreed with Emma. Accidents happened, even in the most aristocratic circles, and I had no intention of letting my friend down by allowing one to happen to her husband.

By the time Bill and I kissed the twins good-bye, I felt fit and ready for service. I was, as Dimity had instructed me to be, prepared for anything.

Anything, that is, except the sight that met my eyes when Hailesham's fabled gardens came into view.

Four

*A*re you sure we're on the right road, Bill?"
I peered intently at the woods lining the narrow, winding lane but didn't see much. A late start, heavy traffic, and the shortening days of early October had left us navigating the back roads of Wiltshire in the dark.

"We passed the lodge gates five minutes ago," Bill replied. "But I'm not sure what to look for next."

"Hailesham House." I cleared my throat and assumed a professorial expression. "A sublime, eighteenth-century neoclassical villa on a hill with three levels of terraced gardens descending from a graceful front staircase to an ornamental lake and a sweeping great lawn. The gardens are open to the public from May to September, but the house is a private residence."

Bill raised an eyebrow. "Excuse me?"

"There're giant topiaries, too," I went on. "Whimsically clipped giant topiaries rising at regular intervals from the yew hedges bordering the lowest level of terraced gardens." I counted on my fingers. "There's a dolphin, a unicorn, a peacock, a turtledove—I'm looking forward to the turtledove."

"Are you making this up?" Bill demanded.

"Would I do that?" I fluttered my eyelashes at him, then grinned. "Emma picked up a brochure at the tourist information office in Oxford. According to the brochure, the ninth Earl Elstyn's primary country residence is surrounded by five hundred acres of forested parkland—so I suppose we *could* be on the right road."

"The land does seem to be forested," Bill agreed.

No sooner had he spoken than the encroaching greenery parted to reveal Lord Elstyn's primary country residence in all its glory. Bill hit the brakes and we sat for a moment in total silence.

"Bill," I said finally. "Do you see what I see?"

"If you mean the flaming turtledove, then yes," Bill replied, "I do."

The giant topiary appeared to be on fire. It was a fantastic sight, as eerie as it was beautiful. Writhing fingers of flame stretched skyward from the whimsically clipped hedges, scattering sparks into the darkness. Burning shreds of shrubbery danced like incandescent butterflies over the ornamental lake while the sublime neoclassical villa hovered serenely above, each windowpane alight with the flickering reflections of the blazing turtledove.

I rested my chin on my hand, mystified. "Do you suppose it's some sort of . . . welcoming gesture?"

"No," Bill said, glancing at the rearview mirror.

"Why not?" I asked.

He tromped on the gas pedal. "Because there's a fire truck coming up behind us."

My teeth rattled as Bill swerved onto the great lawn, and my heart raced as a fleet of fire engines thundered past. Bill waited until the lane was clear, then sped up the graveled drive and skidded to a halt behind the last of the fire trucks. Together we leapt from the Mercedes and ran to the bottom of the graceful staircase. From there I could see a half-dozen men fighting the fire with the tools they had at hand: Two of them trained garden hoses on the surrounding greenery while four others formed a bucket brigade with water dipped from the ornamental lake.

A tall man in a dark, double-breasted suit stood at the top of the staircase, watching, as the professional firefighters went to work with their axes and hoses.

"What's going on?" Bill called up to him.

The man strode down the stairs to join us. I needed no introduction to know who he was. I could see by the light of the burning turtledove that Lord Elstyn resembled his son.

Like Derek, the earl was well over six feet tall, with salt-and-pepper hair and strikingly beautiful midnight-blue eyes, but I detected telling differences as well. Derek's face had been weathered by the elements, but the earl's fair complexion appeared to be lined by age alone. While Derek's curls were as unruly as mine, the earl's had been artfully cut to lie close to his head. Both men had large and capable-looking hands, but Derek's had been roughened by years of manual labor.

The earl's, I soon discovered, were as soft as chamois.

"Bill, dear boy, so good of you to come," said Lord Elstyn. "And you," he added, taking my hand in both of his, "must be Bill's lovely wife. Lori Shepherd, I believe?"

"That's right, my lord," I said. "I'm Lori."

"And I'm Edwin," said the earl. "I refuse to stand on ceremony with the chairwoman of the Westwood Trust." He kissed my hand before releasing it. "I'm delighted to meet you at last and hope one day to meet your splendid sons. I do hope you've brought photographs of them."

It was a bizarre conversation to be having while fire-men were unspooling hose and hacking at shrubbery not fifty yards away, but Dimity had advised me to follow the earl's lead, so I went with the flow.

"No self-respecting mother would leave home without pictures of her children, Lord, er, Edwin." I looked up at him uncertainly. "Do you want to see them now?"

"It might be best to save them for a less hectic moment," he said gently, then turned to Bill. "You had a pleasant journey, I trust?"

Bill pursed his lips. "Your sangfroid is admirable, Lord Elstyn, but mine is wearing thin. Are you going to tell us why your garden's on fire?"

"Sheer carelessness, I should imagine." The earl dismissed the conflagration with a wave of his hand. "I expect we'll discover that one of the gardeners left a tin of paraffin too close to a brush pile. What was supposed to be a small bonfire became instead a rather spectacular display."

I sniffed the air and detected the acrid scent of kerosene.

"The garden will be a bit charred around the edges while you're here," the earl continued, "but I hope the woodland walks will, in some small way, ease your disappointment."

"Are we the first guests to arrive?" I asked, wondering why no one else was outside watching the fire.

"You're the last," the earl informed me. "The others are in their rooms, changing for dinner." He favored me with a warm smile. "I've put you next door to my daughter-in-law. I understand that you're great friends."

He raised his hand, and an elderly man in a dark suit

emerged from the porticoed entryway. He seemed spry despite his years and trotted down the stairs to meet us.

"Giddings will show you to your room, Lori, while I have a brief word with your husband," said the earl.

I glanced over my shoulder, wondering if Giddings was spry enough to handle my ridiculous pile of suitcases, and saw that the Mercedes had vanished.

"Where's our car?" I asked.

"It's been garaged, madam," Giddings informed me. "And your bags are in your room."

The earl's smile found me again. "I won't keep Bill too long," he promised. "In the meantime, if you need anything, anything at all, don't hesitate to ask."

"I won't," I assured him, gave Bill a jaunty wave, and followed Giddings up the stairs.

Under normal circumstances, I might have resented the earl's abrupt usurpation of my husband, but as things stood, I didn't mind it one bit. As far as I was concerned, Lord Elstyn could have as many words with Bill as he liked. I wanted to have a word or two with Emma.

The question foremost in my mind was: Had the topiary been torched to irritate the earl or to send a warning to his undeserving son?

"Accident, my foot," I muttered, glancing back at the turtledove's smoking remains. "No one spills *that* much kerosene."

Hailesham's entrance hall was as cool and formal as a Roman temple, with creamy marble walls, marble statuary—classical nudes conspicuously lacking gooseflesh—and a broad marble staircase with a gold-accented black wrought-iron balustrade. At the second-floor corridor the chilly marble gave way to peach-colored plaster walls, a teak herringbone floor, and soft lighting provided by a series of bronze wall sconces.

My room was halfway down the corridor in the north wing, on the west side of the house. It wouldn't afford me a view of the terraced gardens or the ornamental lake, but its splendor went a long way toward easing my disappointment.

The walls were covered in deep red damask and hung with oil portraits in gilded frames. Layered gold velvet drapes swept back with tasseled cords and topped with gold-fringed swags covered a pair of tall windows, and a glass-paned door gave access to my own private balcony.

The bed was a colossal affair with four barleytwist posts, a carved walnut headboard, and layer upon layer of luxurious bedclothes. I blushed when I spotted Reginald nestled amid the pillows and gave Giddings a sidelong glance, but the old man maintained a neutral expression. I concluded that his job had exposed him to so many outré eccentricities that a powder-pink rabbit seemed tame by comparison.

A dainty writing table sat between the tall windows, and a pair of white-painted doors flanked the bed.

"The door nearest the windows is false," Giddings explained. "It was built for decorative purposes, to balance the other door, which leads to your dressing room."

"My dressing room?" I echoed stupidly.

"Through here, madam," he said, opening the second door.

The dressing room was, if anything, more sumptuous than the bedroom, with a chaise longue, a dressing table, an imposing wardrobe, and an assortment of armchairs, occasional tables, paintings, mirrors, and small bronzes.

"Your dressing room communicates with Mr. Willis's bedroom," said Giddings.

I uttered a highly sophisticated "Huh?"

"Your husband's room is next door," he clarified, pointing to yet another doorway. "The earl felt that such an arrangement might be convenient if Mr. Willis is required to keep unsocial hours."

"We can always leave the doors open," I reasoned.

"As you wish, madam." Giddings directed my attention to the wardrobe. "You will find your clothing in the left-hand compartments. The lavatory is through here."

I followed him into a bathroom that was relatively small but nonetheless complete. My toiletries had been placed beside Bill's on the marble-topped stand between the sink and the claw-footed tub.

Giddings led the way back through the dressing room to my bedroom, where he pointed to the telephone on the bedside table and explained that, if I needed anything at all, I should feel free to ring him.

"Lord Elstyn's guests will assemble in the drawing room, on the ground floor, to the right of the main staircase, at eight o'clock," he concluded.

"Eight?" I glanced at my watch in alarm. "But it's already a quarter-past seven."

"Yes, madam," Giddings said, and left the room.

Short though the time was, I couldn't resist a quick visit to my balcony. It was one of seven projecting from the second story and overlooked a graveled courtyard flanked by outbuildings.

The long, narrow structure to the left appeared to be

the stables, but the row of smaller buildings facing it across the courtyard could have contained anything from a kennel for the hounds to a café for the garden-touring public. I preferred the utilitarian courtyard to the more glamorous terraced gardens. I felt as if I'd been given a privileged peek behind Hailesham's flawless facade.

I left the balcony, checked my watch a second time, and made a snap decision. I'd change first, then slip next door for a quick chat with Emma. It wouldn't do to be late to my first dinner at Hailesham Park.

Five

$\mathcal{F}$ suppose I chose the black dress because I felt a bit intimidated by my surroundings. I wanted to make it clear to my fellow houseguests from the outset that the American lawyer's American wife was someone to be reckoned with.

Besides, I'd been looking forward to seeing Bill's jaw drop.

As I slipped the dress over my head and settled it into place, my own jaw dropped a little. The black dress clung to me like a second skin. It left my shoulders bare and had a slit that reached from my ankle to halfway up my thigh. In the day-to-day routine of motherhood, I'd almost forgotten that I had such a womanly figure. I found myself half hoping that Bill had forgotten, too.

I replaced the heart-shaped locket I usually wore around my neck with a simple floating diamond on a silver chain, then looked for the strappy black sandals I'd planned to wear with my killer dress. I clawed my way through hiking boots, riding boots, sneakers, and bedroom slippers before reaching the heart-sinking conclusion that I'd forgotten to pack a single pair of dress shoes.

"Stupid, stupid, stupid," I muttered, banging myself in the head with a bedroom slipper. I sat back on my heels, then got to my feet. There was no point in sulking. Emma had bought a pair of black pumps in London. They wouldn't be as sexy as the strappy sandals, but they'd be a whole lot closer to the mark than hiking boots.

I padded to the bedroom door, opened it, and peered up and down the corridor. It was deserted. Satisfied that no one would see me scuttling shoeless through Hailesham's hallowed halls, I tiptoed to the bedroom next to mine and knocked frantically.

A man opened the door. He was wearing black trousers, gleaming black shoes, and a snowy-white dress shirt. His black silk bow tie had clearly been tied by hand.

"Hello," he said. "Posting another letter?"

"Uh, no," I said, looking past him in some confusion. "I was expecting to find Emma Harris."

"What a pity." The man leaned casually against the doorjamb, as if he was in no hurry to go anywhere. "If you'd been here thirty minutes ago you would have found her. We swapped rooms."

He was a few years older than I—in his late thirties, at a guess—tall, and well built without being bulky. His dark hair fell in a wave over his high forehead, and his blue eyes were, if anything, even darker and more beautiful than Derek's.

"My balcony overlooked the terraces," he was saying. "When I learned of Emma's interest in gardening, I insisted that she have the better view."

"Th-that was very kind of you," I managed, trying not to stare at the pair of boyish dimples that punctuated his smile.

"Not at all. I find my current view extremely satisfying." As he spoke, his glorious eyes traveled slowly from my décolletage to my feet, which were attempting in vain to hide behind each other. "Poor Cinders! You've lost your glass slippers."

I laughed through my blushes and said quickly, "It's not a fashion statement. I forgot to pack my good shoes. I was hoping Emma would help me out."

"I'm sure she will. She's at the end of the corridor." The man's gaze made a slow return journey to my face. "I'm Simon Elstyn, by the way."

I licked my lips and decided that it was high time for me to stop behaving like a starstruck teenager. "I'm Lori Shepherd," I said evenly. "I'm married to Bill Willis, one of Lord Elstyn's attorneys."

"What a coincidence," said Simon. "I, too, am married to one of Lord Elstyn's attorneys." He leaned closer and purred, "I expect they'll be extremely busy this week. Whatever shall we do with our free time?"

My mouth fell open. "You're kidding, right?"

"Sorry?" he said, looking mildly disconcerted.

I tilted my head to one side and eyed him doubtfully. "I've heard that married people are supposed to play the field during country-house weekends, but I guess I expected the invitations to be a little more subtle. Honestly, Simon, if you had a mustache, you'd be twirling it."

Amusement lit his eyes. "I was under the impression that Americans were impervious to subtlety."

"You've been misinformed." I turned to leave, but my curiosity got the better of me. "What you said before, about delivering a letter—what did you mean?"

"Someone's been playing post office." His eyes twinkled as he added, "I must say that I'm glad it's not you."

"Right. Well . . ." I backed away, too dazzled by his

smile to question him further. "Better go find some shoes."

"If you need anything else," he said, "feel free to knock on my door. Anytime."

"Uh, thanks," I stammered, and as I walked to the end of the long corridor, I could feel him watching me every step of the way.

I was so distracted by the sensation that I nearly barreled into Emma as she and Derek emerged from the last door on the right. Derek was dressed in a tuxedo that had, by the looks of it, only recently come out of hibernation, but Emma was resplendent in a floor-length silver-gray gown with a matching bolero jacket and—I noted with relief—a pair of pearl-gray flats.

"You made it!" Emma exclaimed. "I thought you'd never get here."

"We were held up by traffic and I'm in desperate need of shoes," I blurted.

Emma peered down at my feet, shook her head in mock despair, and went back into the room.

"Everything all right, Lori?" asked Derek. "You look flushed."

"I'm fine," I said, putting Simon's smile firmly out of my mind, "though I'm dying to know how the topiary caught fire."

Derek harrumphed. "Disaffected peasants, I should imagine."

"Seriously?" I asked, wide-eyed.

"Of course not." Derek looked at me askance, then drew a picture in the air with his index finger. "The lower terrace is bordered by a wrought-iron balustrade. The blacksmith was soldering a joint near the shrubbery this afternoon. He must have let a spark fly into the bushes, where it smoldered until it flared up in the evening breeze. It's a pity."

"It's a tragedy," Emma corrected as she returned to the corridor, black pumps in hand. "Do you have any idea how long it takes to cultivate large-scale topiaries? Thank heavens the unicorn and the peacock were spared."

"Are you sure about your facts, Derek?" I asked, slipping into Emma's shoes. "Your father seems to think——"

"Father hasn't bothered to speak with the blacksmith," Derek interrupted. "Manual laborers are beneath his notice. Arrogant old fool."

"Derek . . ." Emma pleaded.

"All right." Derek held his hands up to pacify his wife. "I'll behave myself. If he will."

Emma sighed resignedly. "It's almost eight. We'd better go down."

I walked gingerly behind them, testing the fit of Emma's pumps and puzzling over Derek's words. I hadn't noticed an evening breeze when I'd stood watching the fire, but I had detected the distinctive scent of kerosene. "Derek," I began, "what about the——"

"Cousin Derek!"

I looked up and saw Simon Elstyn striding toward us, smiling his devastating smile.

"Good evening, Si." Derek's greeting was somewhat less than enthusiastic. "Lori, this is my cousin——"

"We've met," I said. "Simon told me where to find you."

"Always glad to help a damsel in distress." Simon bowed gallantly and turned to Derek. "A small reminder, Cousin——your father's an Edwardian at heart. He frowns mightily on husbands who escort their wives into dinner."

He offered his arm to Emma, adding smoothly, "It's absurd, I know, but when in Rome . . ."

Emma glanced uncertainly at Derek, then took Simon's arm. "Thank you, Simon. We seem to be short one husband."

"I'm sure he and Gina will catch us up at dinner," said Simon, leading her toward the staircase.

"Gina?" I whispered, slipping my hand into the crook of Derek's arm.

"Georgina Elstyn," he replied quietly. "Simon's wife. She works for my father. She's—"

"An attorney," I murmured, and lapsed into a preoccupied silence.

It had suddenly occurred to me that Gina might be one of the intermediaries who'd met with Bill to conduct the earl's legal business at the London office of Willis & Willis. If she were, then Bill had worked with her for the past three months, without mentioning it to me. Had he known that she would be at Hailesham Park?

"I don't suppose you'd consider coming out with me for a bag of fish and chips," Derek murmured gloomily. "I tried to talk Emma into it, but—"

"Sorry, old bean, but wild horses couldn't keep me from this dinner." I grasped his arm firmly and squared my over-exposed shoulders. If Gina Elstyn was as attractive as her husband, then Derek wouldn't be the only one I'd watch closely for the next five days.

The drawing room split the difference between the entrance hall's chilly classicism and my bedroom's opulent warmth. The architecture was cool and classical: The off-white walls held a quartet of pilasters that rose from the floor to a white-on-white frieze encircling the room, and the barrel-vaulted ceiling was pierced with a pattern of octagonal medallions. Two unadorned Doric columns at the far end of the room separated the main section from an alcove containing a grand piano and a half-dozen shield-back chairs.

The fireplace looked like a miniature Greek temple. The oil portrait over the mantelshelf was framed by a pair of diminutive Doric columns supporting a triangular pediment, and the creamy marble surround was carved with scrolls and abstract acanthus leaves.

The hearth was flanked by two lacquered commodes that faced a pair of French doors opening onto a stone-flagged terrace. A rosewood secretaire filled the space between the French doors, and an inlaid drum table sat between a pair of round-backed armchairs. An Aubusson carpet and a sparkling chandelier lent warmth to the room, as did the coral damask settee sitting at a right angle to the hearth.

Lord Elstyn was chatting with a young woman on the settee when we arrived. The young woman wore her white-blond hair in a spiky crew cut, and she was dressed in an electric-blue gown that covered her from neck to toes yet left nothing whatsoever to the imagination. If my dress fit like a glove, hers looked as if it had been sprayed on.

The young woman remained seated as we entered the room, but the earl rose from the settee to greet us.

"Lori, Emma, welcome. I see you've met Simon." He beamed at Emma's escort, but his eyes merely grazed

Derek's face. "Simon's my brother Kenneth's eldest son. His other son is Oliver." The earl turned toward a young man standing near the grand piano. "Oliver, stop lurking in the shadows," he called. "I wish to introduce you to Ms. Shepherd and Lady Hailesham."

Derek clenched his fists, but Emma's warning look and my grip on his arm restrained him from registering any complaint he might have had about his wife's correct name.

"There's no need for titles among family," Emma said, with remarkable aplomb. "Please call me Emma."

"As you wish," said the earl, with a courtly bow.

Oliver Elstyn was in his midthirties—about my age—and not quite as tall as his brother. His hair was dark, but it was hard to tell the color of his eyes because he scarcely lifted his gaze from the carpet as he shook Emma's hand, then turned to me.

"How do you do, Ms. Shepherd?" he said, so softly I almost didn't hear him.

"Very well, thank you," I replied. His handshake was as gentle as his voice. "But I'll do much better if you call me Lori."

I caught a flash of midnight blue as his eyes met mine, but he quickly lowered them again when the earl spoke.

"Allow me to present Lady Landover, my brother Thomas's only child." The earl beckoned to the young woman, who got to her feet and strolled over to join us. "Claudia's husband is unable to be with us this week, which is just as well. I detest an odd number at dinner."

Claudia Landover emitted a shrill laugh. "What an awful thing to say, Uncle. Married women miss their husbands dreadfully when they're away, don't we, Lori?"

"Yes," I replied, a shade dishonestly. Bill was away so often that there were times when I hardly realized he was gone. I was, however, keenly aware of the fact that neither he nor the mysterious Gina was present in the drawing room.

Claudia drew me over to sit on the settee, Derek and Oliver retreated to the alcove, and the earl and Simon took Emma to the French doors to look out.

"You're not wearing makeup!" Claudia exclaimed. She had a voice like a Klaxon. "How extraordinary!"

Her comment brought a rush of color to my face that would have rendered blusher redundant.

"I don't care for makeup," I said shortly. "I find it uncomfortable."

"Uncomfortable?" Claudia's Elstyn-blue eyes registered incomprehension.

"It limits my range of motion," I explained. "I like to be able to rub my nose without worrying about smearing my fingers with paint."

"I'll admit it's inconvenient at times," Claudia allowed, "but I've always thought it a form of politeness to make the best of oneself when appearing in public."

I didn't think Claudia was being catty. I didn't think she was intelligent enough to be catty, and if I hadn't been feeling peevish about Bill's absence, I would have let her off the hook and changed the subject. But my bad temper got the better of me, and before I could stop myself I let her have it with both barrels.

"I've always thought it more polite to tell the truth," I said.

Claudia leaned back. "I beg your pardon?"

"Makeup's a lie," I snapped. "It's a way of saying, 'I'm younger, older, paler, rosier than I really am.'" I stared pointedly at her bleached crew cut. "The same goes for hair coloring, which I also don't use, because, as with most lies, once you start telling it, the harder it is to stop. I prefer not to start."

"Bravo, Lori." Unbeknownst to me, Simon had left Emma with the earl and crossed to stand close enough to overhear the whole ridiculous tirade. "Makeup's inconvenient for men as well. One kiss and we're marked for life." His gaze lingered on my lips. "I'm delighted to hear that you don't wear it."

"I think you're both quite mad," Claudia declared.

The drawing room door opened and Bill appeared, dressed in his flawless dinner jacket, with a slim, dark-haired woman on his arm. She was wearing a beautifully cut black gown with long sleeves and a modest décolletage. If Bill's jaw dropped when he saw me, I didn't notice. I had eyes only for his companion.

"Gina!" Claudia called. "What would you say about a woman who refuses to wear makeup?"

"I'd say she's either very beautiful"—Gina's voice was distressingly low and musical—"or very foolish."

"I know how I'd cast my vote," Simon murmured from the corner of his mouth.

After introducing Gina and me to each other, the earl announced, "The party is complete, or nearly so. Oliver, take Emma in to dinner."

Simon bent low to address me. "Would you do me the honor, madam?"

I glanced once at Bill, stood, and took Simon's arm, saying grimly, "You bet."

Derek paired up with Claudia, and the earl led the procession into the entrance hall, where he paused to gaze up the marble staircase.

The rest of us paused, too, and were rewarded with an unforgettable sight.

The Honorable Eleanor Harris had arrived.

Six

ell Harris had always been unforgettable. Some said her mother's early death and Derek's years of grief had shaped her character, but Dimity, who'd known Nell as a child, disagreed.

Nell would have been exactly who she is, no matter what the circumstances, she'd once told me. *Nell is an old soul. She was born knowing more than you or I will ever learn.*

Dimity's words came back to me as I beheld Nell on the staircase. She was breathtaking—tall and willowy and as ethereally beautiful as a fairy queen, with an aureole of golden curls to serve as her crown.

The gown she wore was from another age, ivory silk falling in tiny pleats from a high-waisted bodice embroidered with seed pearls and trimmed with the merest whisper of lace. She'd threaded a pale blue satin ribbon through her curls but wore no jewelry. She needed none. Her hair shone like liquid gold and her blue eyes would have put the finest sapphires to shame.

Nell surveyed us with the grace and self-possession of a woman who would one day rule the world. It was hard to believe she'd not yet reached her seventeenth birthday.

"Good evening," she said.

"Good evening," we chorused, a herd of serfs rendered pliant by her majesty.

Ivory satin slippers peeped from beneath her hem as she descended the staircase. "I apologize for my tardiness. Bertie was unwell."

Bertie was the chocolate-brown teddy bear who accompanied Nell everywhere. Nell's affection for her bear tempted fools to underestimate her, but they soon learned—usually the hard way—that Nell's myriad eccentricities concealed a formidable intelligence.

"Bertie was frightened by the fire," Nell continued. "Have you discovered who set it?"

"The fire wasn't set deliberately, Nell," said Derek. "The blacksmith was soldering——"

"It was an accident," Lord Elstyn interrupted. "Tell Bertie there's nothing to worry about."

"Isn't there?" Nell gazed intently at Simon, nodded to me and Bill, then moved forward to embrace her father and stepmother, murmuring, "Mama, Papa, I'm so glad you're here."

"Yes," the earl said gruffly. "We're all pleased that you've come, my boy. It's been far too long since we've dined together as a family."

Derek stared at his father, clearly at a loss for words, but Nell saved him the trouble of responding.

Her hand came to rest on the earl's arm as lightly as a tuft of down. "Shall we go in?"

The dining room could have been plastered with peanut butter and I wouldn't have noticed. I was too busy stealing glances at my husband.

Bill and I were seated as far away from each other as it was possible to be, on opposite ends and sides of the enormous mahogany table. Gina sat beside him. They seemed to be enjoying themselves, chatting and laughing with the familiarity of old friends. Their chummy behavior put to rest any doubts I had about the length of their acquaintance.

I sat between Lord Elstyn and Simon, and when I wasn't spying on my husband, I was listening to the men's conversation. It was clear that the earl was proud of his nephew, and with good reason: Simon sat on the boards of at least three major corporations and twice as many charities. Both men were remarkably well informed on the Westwood Trust's various projects and drew from me an enthusiatic account of the work being done at St. Benedict's, the trust-supported homeless shelter in Oxford.

"You go there yourself?" the earl asked.

I nodded. "I've worked my way up to pot scrubber."

"Remarkable," the earl murmured.

"Admirable," Simon stated firmly.

Even while we spoke, a part of my mind was focused on the end of the meal when, if the earl lived up to his Edwardian reputation, the ladies would be banished to the drawing room while the gentlemen stayed behind to pass the decanter.

Sure enough, when the last plate had been cleared, the ladies rose as one—apart from me and Emma, who rose somewhat belatedly—and left the men to their port. Emma attempted to catch my eye when we entered the drawing room, but Claudia intercepted her and dragged her over to the fireplace.

I made a beeline for Gina Elstyn.

"So," I said brightly. "You're Gina."

"And you're Lori." Gina had hazel eyes and her chin-length brown hair was straight and shiny and held back from her face by an elegant brown velvet band. Her wedding ring had a rock on it the size of Pike's Peak. "Bill's told me so much about you."

"Has he?" I lifted an eyebrow. "He hasn't told me a thing about you."

"Good." Gina spoke with the chilly detachment of a polished professional. "My uncle has strict rules about confidentiality. He insists that our business meetings be conducted in complete secrecy."

"I hate to be the one to break it to you, Gina, but the secret's out." I gestured toward Claudia, Emma, and Nell, who were clustered in conversation around the hearth. "The Elstyns are here, one big happy family, except that they're not, are they? Why haven't the aunts and uncles joined in the fun? Why has the earl focused on the younger generation? What's going on?"

"I'm not at liberty to answer your questions, Lori," Gina replied. "I work for my uncle, you see, and I play by his rules."

"Gina!" Claudia's voice could have been heard in the next county. "We're completely outnumbered. Nell and Emma agree with Lori about makeup."

"Oh, Lord," I muttered, rubbing my temples.

Gina turned toward the others, but before she could reply, the door opened and Simon came into the room. He went directly to his wife and told her that she was wanted in the dining room. She gave me a cool nod and departed, but Simon stayed behind.

"If Claudia says one more word about makeup," I

growled through gritted teeth, "I'm going to stab her to death with an eyebrow pencil."

"Fresh air?" Simon suggested.

"Please," I replied gratefully, and we exited through the French doors.

In my haste to escape Claudia's clutches I'd forgotten that it was October and that my black dress wasn't suited to the great outdoors. I began to shiver the moment the cool night air touched my skin.

Simon noticed, removed his dress jacket, and draped it around my shoulders. He would have left his arm there, too, if I hadn't walked away. He caught up with me in two strides, offered his elbow instead, and guided me toward a short flight of stone steps that descended into the uppermost of the three terraced gardens.

The fire brigade had long since gone. The night was still and silent save for the muted murmur of voices coming from the drawing room. A nearly full moon cast a soft glow over the shadowy landscape as we strolled along a grassy path bordered by formal flowerbeds that had been tucked up for the winter.

"Is the path smooth enough for Emma's shoes?" Simon inquired.

"It's like a billiards table," I told him. "I could dance a minuet on it in Emma's shoes—if I knew how to dance a minuet."

"I'll teach you," he offered.

I stopped short. "Do you really know how to dance a minuet?"

"I do," he said. "I was taught it by a dancing master, here, in the ballroom, when I was eleven years old."

I looked him up and down. "You're remarkably well

preserved for someone who was born in the eighteenth century."

Simon laughed. "I freely admit to being out of step with my time. I've always preferred the country to the city, the handmade to the mass-produced, the minuet to the . . ." He frowned. "Do dances have names nowadays?"

"If they do, I don't know what they are," I replied.

"We're in the rose garden," Simon informed me as we walked on. "In June the air is intoxicating, but I'm afraid it's rather less so in October."

"Still," I said, "it's a beautiful place."

"It's more beautiful in June." Simon stopped beneath an elaborate wrought-iron arch, and an intricate pattern of shadows fell on his upturned face. "When the climbing roses are in bloom, it's the most beautiful place on earth."

"Emma might agree with you," I allowed, "but I'm not sure about Derek. I don't think he cares much for Haile-sham Park."

"He never did," said Simon. "Even as a child, he pre-ferred the carpenter's shed to the house." He ran a finger-tip along a wrought-iron curlicue. "You know my cousin fairly well, Lori. Has he ever told you why he so thor-oughly dislikes his home?"

"He and his father don't seem to get along," I said diplomatically.

"Even if I thought my uncle the worst tyrant in the world, I could never hate Hailesham," said Simon. "There must be some other explanation."

I thought of the cheerful disorder that reigned in Derek's manor house and compared it to Hailesham's un-cluttered perfection. I pictured Derek's muddy work boots, glanced at Simon's gleaming black shoes, and swept a hand through the air to indicate the manicured flower-beds surrounding us.

"Maybe he considers it a bit . . . elitist," I ventured.

"Elitist?" Simon's mouth tightened, and though he spoke quietly, his voice was taut with anger. "Are beauty, craftsmanship, and continuity elitist? Hailesham wasn't run off on an assembly line. It was made by hand. It was created by masons, joiners, painters, plasterers—men who strove for a kind of self-expression rendered obsolete by soulless modern architecture." He grasped the wrought-iron arch as if to reassure himself of its permanence. "I should think Derek, of all people, would appreciate the distinction."

"I'm sure he does," I began, but Simon didn't seem to be listening.

"Hundreds of country houses were demolished in the last century," he went on. "Treasure houses the likes of which will never be seen again. It's a miracle that Hailesham survived, a miracle wrought by succeeding generations of my family who cared enough to . . ." He tossed his head in disgust. "Does Derek realize how many craftsmen we employ to maintain the house?"

"Simon," I said gently. "Forget that I mentioned the word *elitist*. It was an idiotic thing to say. Derek's devoted his life to restoring old buildings. No one appreciates craftsmanship more than he does."

Simon released the arch and held his hand out to me beseechingly. "Then why does he hate the place?"

"I don't know." I clasped his hand. "But it's clear to me that you love it."

Simon's anger seemed to fade. He took a deep breath,

caught his lower lip between his teeth, and regarded me shamefacedly. "Forgive me," he said. "I'm being a bore. Gina finds nothing more tedious than my passionate defense of Hailesham Park."

"I don't think you're boring," I said stoutly. "I mean, it's not just a home you're defending, it's . . . it's *civilization*— a handmade world as opposed to one built by machines. If defending civilization doesn't rouse your passions, I don't know what will."

Simon gazed at me gravely for a heartbeat or two, then his dimples showed and his blue eyes twinkled mischievously. "I can think of at least one other thing that rouses my passion. Shall I tell you?"

I couldn't help smiling as his flirtatious mask slipped back into place, though I felt a bit sorry for him, too. I was beginning to suspect that he used the mask as protective coloration in a world where true passion was dismissed as tedious.

"I'm pretty sure I can guess," I said dryly. I released his hand and walked to the low stone wall bordering the rose garden. I stopped at a spot that afforded a good view of the turtledove's former perch. The scent of kerosene had dissipated, but the topiary's charred remains were still very much in evidence.

I gazed thoughtfully at the blackened, soggy mess. Derek and the earl believed that the fire had been an unfortunate accident, but I still had my doubts. Could sheer coincidence explain the destruction of one of Hailesham's prized topiaries within hours of Derek's arrival, or was something more sinister at work? The ornamental figures were in plain view of the house, but the hedges containing them were high enough to allow anyone to light a fire and escape unseen, especially after dark.

"Has Gina told you why we're here?" I asked.

Simon came to stand beside me. He peered silently toward the blurred line of distant woods for a moment, then bent forward to prop his elbows on the wall.

"Gina never tells me anything," he said softly. "She seldom has time to spare for conversation. Her work requires her to be away from home quite often. It's all highly confidential."

I glanced at him uncertainly. I'd expected an evasive or a playful answer. His directness had caught me off guard and his words had struck closer to home than he could have realized. I, too, was married to a high-powered professional who disappeared for weeks on end to conduct business about which he seldom spoke. It was like being married to a spy. I studied Simon's profile, wondering what else we had in common.

"Do you have children?" I asked.

"A son," he said. "He's at Eton. You?"

"Twin boys," I told him. "They're at home with their nanny."

"Aren't we lucky?" Simon turned his head to gaze at me. The sadness in his eyes touched me more deeply than I was willing to admit.

I folded my arms inside his jacket and looked away. "It must have broken your heart to see the topiary burn."

"It was meant to," he said.

I looked at him sharply. "Excuse me?"

Simon stared straight ahead. "The fire was no accident, Lori. I believe it was set intentionally, to intimidate me." His lips quirked into a wry smile as he added, "Not only because I'm the perfect egoist, but because of a curious item I found in my room shortly after I arrived."

I cast my mind back to my first encounter with Simon. He'd said something then that had piqued my curiosity: *"Someone's been playing post office. . . ."*

"A letter?" I guessed.

"You've a retentive memory, Lori." Simon straightened. "Someone left it on my dressing table. I found it before I exchanged rooms with Emma, so there's no doubt it was meant for me. Care to see it?"

I eyed him narrowly. "Are you telling the truth, Simon, or is this a ploy to get me up to your bedroom?"

"Would I need a ploy?" He didn't wait for an answer but gestured toward his jacket. "I didn't think it wise to leave the note lying about, so I brought it with me. You'll find it in the inside breast pocket."

I slid my hand into the jacket's pocket and removed a folded half-sheet of plain white paper. I opened it and held it up to the moonlight.

"Good grief," I muttered.

It was a classic poison-pen note. The words were made up of individual letters clipped from books and pasted together in three crooked lines:

watch the birdie.
it could happen to you.
leave hailesham or it will.

I shuddered and when Simon put his arm around me this time, I didn't move away.

"It's horrible," I said. "You should take it to the police."

He gently pulled the threatening note from my hand. "Elstyns solve their problems privately," he said quietly. "My uncle abhors the thought of public scandal."

"Have you shown it to Gina?" I asked.

He gave a mirthless chuckle. "She's been far too busy to spare a moment for her husband."

I looked up at him, bewildered. "Why are you telling me about it?"

"We're birds of a feather, you and I." He leaned his head closer to mine. "And I need someone who knows her way around a library."

My bewilderment increased. I couldn't imagine how he'd learned that I'd once worked as a rare-book bibliographer in my alma mater's library.

He seemed to read my mind. "Your husband was singing your praises over the port."

The idea of Bill bragging about me in front of the earl filled me with delight. In an instant all of his sins—including those he hadn't yet committed—were forgiven.

"Was he?" I said, beaming.

"Incessantly." Simon cocked an ear toward the house as Claudia's shrill voice announced the return of the men and Gina to the drawing room. His hold on me tightened. "Meet me in the library tomorrow at nine. Tell no one."

A thousand questions clamored to be asked, but there was no time. I hastily returned his jacket and smoothed my rumpled dress.

"I'll be there," I promised. "And, Simon"—I gripped his arm—"be careful."

He stared at my hand for a moment, then reached out to touch me lightly on the cheek. "Too late for that, I'm afraid."

The air seemed to tingle between us. My hand slid from his arm and I headed for the drawing room without saying another word. I didn't trust myself to speak. I could laugh at Simon's flirting, but his sincerity was more than I could handle.

Seven

*B*ill was so tired by the time we got upstairs that he tumbled into his own bed without pausing to ask how my evening had gone. I stood over him for a while, then bent low to kiss him, hoping he'd murmur my name, but the only name he whispered was *"Gina."*

I fell back a step, too stunned to speak, and quickly told myself that it meant nothing. Bill had spent most of the evening with his colleague; it was only natural that she should be on his mind. I ordered myself not to overreact, then retreated to my room to speak with Dimity.

It was nearly two in the morning and the fire in my hearth was burning low. I sat atop the bedclothes with Reginald perched on a pillow beside me and the blue journal open in my lap, determined not to mention what had just happened.

"We were wrong, Dimity," I said. "It's not Derek who needs a bodyguard, it's Simon." I pulled Reginald closer to me as the lines of royal-blue ink began to curl and loop across the page.

Simon Elstyn, eldest son of Edwin's brother Kenneth?

"That's right," I said. "He's married to Gina, and his brother's name is Oliver."

I remember Simon. He was Edwin's favorite. He and Oliver spent all of their holidays at Hailesham.

"Did you like Simon?" I asked.

Who could help liking Simon?

The question begged for laughter, but I could only manage a wan smile. "Whoever's threatening to kill him, for a start."

I'm sorry?

I shoved all thoughts of Bill and Gina to the back of my mind and concentrated on telling Dimity about the poison-pen letter and the torched topiary.

It would certainly hurt Simon to hurt Hailesham. He loved it here when he was a boy.

"He loves it even more, now that he's grown up." I thought for a moment, then went on. "Nell Harris seems to connect the fire to Simon, too. When Edwin told her not to worry about it, she gave Simon one of her meaningful looks."

Nell's skilled at reading people, as I'm sure you've discovered. What's your opinion?

"It's arson," I said bluntly. "I could smell kerosene from fifty yards away. If you combine arson with a death threat, it's hard to avoid the conclusion that Simon's being singled out for harassment." I reached over to twiddle Reginald's ears. "I wonder if he's up to something or if the letter-writer's just plain crazy."

It could be a bit of both. Simon was a charming boy, but he had a streak of mischief in him as well. He rather enjoyed disconcerting people.

"He still does," I said, recalling the touch of his fingertips on my face.

Ask Simon if he knows why the writer objects so strenuously to his presence at Hailesham. I doubt that he'll give you a straight answer, but ask nonetheless.

"I intend to." I looked toward the balcony. "It must be an inside job, Dimity."

I agree. Edwin's always been a stickler for security. A stranger would find it difficult to flit about the property unnoticed. There was a pause as Dimity collected her thoughts. *Has anyone else received a nasty letter? You might inquire. You should also make it your business to discover who had the opportunity to deliver the letter to Simon's room.*

"I suppose one of the servants could have done it," I said, "or any of the others who arrived before he did. I'll find out."

Have you told Bill about the death threat?

"No," I said, and hurried on. "He's been really busy since we arrived and he was exhausted when we finally came upstairs, and if I told him, he'd *insist* on calling the police."

True. As an attorney, Bill's accustomed to utilizing official resources. He might even be correct in doing so. A death threat should never be taken lightly, Lori.

"I'm not taking it lightly," I said. "I'm respecting Simon's wishes. He asked me not to tell anyone about it."

Simon asked you to keep a secret from your husband? And you agreed? Dimity didn't write *tsk, tsk,* but I could almost hear her clucking her tongue. *Tread carefully, Lori. You've walked this path before.*

I was sorely tempted to tell her that my husband had fallen asleep with another woman's name on his lips, but I kept silent. How could I question Bill's behavior when my own track record was less than spotless? I'd never been unfaithful to him—in the strictest sense of the word—

but Dimity knew that I'd had more than my share of close calls. She was tactfully reminding me of my unfortunate susceptibility to charming men to whom I was not married.

"I'll be okay," I assured her. "Simon's such a flagrant flirt that I'd be embarrassed to be seduced by him."

Three cheers for self-respect. Now, tell me, what did you have for dinner?

"For dinner?" I blinked, surprised by the change of subject, then remembered that Dimity was supposed to be enjoying a carefree holiday. "Consommé, poached salmon, roast partridge, white asparagus, lemon sorbet, treacle tart, fresh peaches, and the usual assortment of wines and cheeses."

Treacle tart? An unusual choice for such a formal meal, but I'm sure it was delicious. In my day, Edwin was known far and wide for the splendor of his table. I'm glad to know that high standards still prevail. Did he use the family dinner service?

"The china was marked with the Elstyn crest, if that's what you mean," I said.

Lovely. And were you able to cope with the partridge?

"I poked the knife into the joints, the way you told me to, and the legs just fell off." I frowned in puzzlement. "Why do you suppose Simon wants me to meet him in the library?"

Isn't it obvious, my dear? He wants your help in finding the books vandalized by the poison pen.

I chided myself for not catching on more quickly, then remembered that I hadn't been thinking very clearly when I'd left the rose garden.

It seems our holiday at Hailesham Park will be every bit as adventurous as you predicted. You must promise me that you'll con-

duct your investigation with the utmost caution. Poison pens are notoriously unstable. If ours discovers that you're in league with Simon, he may come after you as well.

Her warning tweaked my curiosity. "Has anyone ever sent you a death threat, Dimity?"

Yes, once, long ago. It's an occupational hazard for anyone with wealth.

I nodded thoughtfully. "What did you do about it?"

I turned it over to Scotland Yard. They never discovered who sent it. But I did.

I sat up, intrigued. "Who was it?"

One of my most trusted assistants. She made the mistake of clipping letters from a report issued by the Westwood Trust. The typeface was unusual and the report had a limited circulation. It didn't require much delving to reveal the culprit's identity.

"Did you turn her in to the police?" I asked.

I had no choice but to inform the authorities. She'd become dangerously deranged, Lori, which is why I want you to be on guard.

"I'll watch my step," I promised.

In the meantime, I suggest that you turn the light out and get some rest. You must be alert tomorrow.

"Good night, Dimity."

Sleep well, my dear.

I waited until her words had faded from the page, then set the journal and Reginald on the bedside table, climbed under the covers, and switched off the light. I leaned back against the mound of pillows and gazed silently at the wall that separated my room from Simon's.

I was glad he'd come to me with the threatening letter. I'd been looking forward to guarding Derek, but the prospect of taking an active role in Simon's investigation was more appealing still. There was a certain thrill in knowing that a madman—or madwoman—walked among us.

Who would it be? I wondered. Who hated the likable Simon enough to attempt to drive him away from the grand reunion?

Derek's was the first name that came to mind. My friend didn't seem overly fond of his cousin, and had reason to resent him. While Derek was the earl's estranged and hostile son, Simon was the earl's favorite. As such, he posed a potential threat to Derek's inheritance.

"No, Reg, it can't be Derek," I said, glancing at my pink bunny. "He's not sneaky enough. I can picture him punching Simon in the nose maybe, but I can't see him pasting together an anonymous death threat. It must be someone else."

Could Claudia be the culprit? I asked myself. It was difficult to imagine clueless Claudia plotting anything more complex than a shopping spree, but there might be more to her than met the eye.

Then there was Oliver, the bashful younger brother who'd grown up in Simon's shadow. Truckloads of demented resentments could spring from being ignored, overlooked, and dismissed as second best. Perhaps Oliver had finally had enough. Perhaps he'd decided to grab some of the spotlight for himself by casting a shadow over Simon. Oliver was a definite possibility.

Last, but not least, there was Gina. Had she grown tired of watching her husband offer his arm—and who knew what else?—to other women? Had she sent the death threat to punish him? Or was someone else wandering the halls, unknown to the rest of us?

I pulled the covers up to my chin and gazed into the

fire. I'd never admit it to Dimity, but the thought of spending more time alone with Simon held a certain thrill as well. I wasn't drawn to him simply because of his beguiling manner or his enchanting good looks, or even because I needed someone to distract me from whatever might be going on between my husband and his wife.

In truth, I felt a sense of kinship with him. We were both out of step with the vulgar, mass-produced, disposable world into which we'd been born. My cottage might be humbler that Hailesham, but I treasured every hand-hewn joist and floorboard. On a more personal level, we share the fate of spouses who were left alone too often, and we were, each of us, passionate creatures.

I couldn't forget the tender look he'd given me when I'd urged him to be careful. He hadn't been playacting. His suave mask had fallen away, revealing the face of a man so starved for affection that a simple gesture of concern caught at his heart. It seemed pathetic that a man with so much charm could be so lonely.

"Poor little rich boy," I murmured. "Could it be that you have everything you desire except someone who cares about you?"

I rolled onto my side and looked at Reginald. His black button eyes gleamed softly in the dying firelight.

"Simon thinks that he and I are birds of a feather, Reg, but he's wrong. Poor Simon's stuck with Gina, while I've got my own sweet Bill." I frowned distractedly at the faded grape-juice stain on my bunny's snout. "At least I *think* I've got him. . . ."

Eight

Oliver Elstyn was alone in the dining room when I went down for breakfast. Bill had risen at an ungodly hour to spend the morning huddled with Gina, Derek, and Lord Elstyn in the earl's study, but I'd slept until half-past seven before showering and getting dressed. I intended to carry on as if I'd never heard Bill whisper Gina's name.

Dimity had directed me to a demure twinset and a tweed skirt in heathery shades of green and lavender. The conservative outfit made me feel like a country-house veteran, and I was relieved to see that Oliver's clothes were equally informal: a herringbone tweed jacket over a beige shirt, and brown wool trousers.

"Where is everyone?" I asked, noting the empty chairs.

Oliver looked up from his food. "Emma, Nell, and Claudia have gone riding and Simon's gone with them. He's putting his new hunter through its paces."

He nodded toward the twelve-paned windows and I saw a row of ivy-covered hurdles on the great lawn. As I scanned the grounds, four riders came into view, galloping along the edge of the ornamental lake. Three rode past the hurdles, but the fourth, a tall figure on a huge dappled gray, sailed easily over the first hurdle and took the rest without breaking stride.

I thought the lead rider must be Simon but couldn't be sure. I recognized Emma as the shortest of the four, but at a distance the cousins were indistinguishable—long-legged, slender, and dressed in black velvet helmets, tall black boots, fawn breeches, and black riding coats.

"Better them than me," I said, shaking my head. "Riding's right up there with emergency dental work on my list of favorite activities."

The quip won a tentative smile from Simon's younger brother.

"You're not fond of horses?" he inquired.

"I'm fond of them," I said, "as long as I don't have to climb up on them."

"My uncle will be disappointed," Oliver commented. "He believes riding to be an essential skill for every gentlewoman."

I snorted derisively. "Scratch me off the gentlewoman list, then. I'll get over it."

Oliver gave me a searching look, then nodded once, as if in approval. "If you'd like fresh tea or coffee . . ."

"I'll be fine with what's here." I turned to survey the silver serving dishes crowding the sideboard. "Your uncle must have a shipload of galley slaves down in the kitchen."

Oliver shrugged diffidently. "The regular staff's not as large as you might expect. Uncle Edwin takes on extra help when he has guests."

He seemed almost apologetic, as if he were embarrassed by his uncle's aristocratic lifestyle. I wondered if he shared Derek's aversion to conspicuous consumption.

I loaded a plate with kippers, scrambled eggs, fried tomatoes, and kedgeree and took a seat across from Oliver. It was the perfect opportunity to ask if he'd received a poison-pen letter, but I wasn't sure how to go about it. It wasn't a subject that came up often in everyday conversation.

"Enjoying the reunion?" I began.

"Not much." Oliver shrugged. "I manage my uncle's portfolio. I'm better with paperwork than with people."

"Even when it's family?" I said.

"Especially when it's family," he murmured.

I raised a forkful of kedgeree. "Did you all travel down together?"

Oliver looked as though I'd asked him to juggle the kippers.

"We *never* travel together," he assured me. "I like to arrive early, Claudia always runs late, and Simon and Gina prefer absolute punctuality."

"So you got here first," I prompted, fixing the timetable in my head.

"Yes," he replied. "Though Cousin Nell was here before me. I believe she arrived from Paris two nights ago. Uncle Edwin sent the car to fetch her from Heathrow."

While Oliver addressed his fried eggs, I ruminated. If Oliver had his facts straight, the Honorable Nell Harris—Derek's darling daughter and the apple of Lord Elstyn's eye—had arrived at Hailesham Park two days ago, in plenty of time to create the poison-pen letter and deliver it to Simon's room. She could have torched the turtledove as well.

I thought back to Nell descending the grand staircase as we crossed the entrance hall the night before. She'd been the last to come down to dinner. Had she been busy comforting her pyrophobic teddy bear, as she'd claimed? Or had she been scrubbing the stink of kerosene from her clothes?

I remembered, too, the strange look she'd given Simon when Lord Elstyn had declared the fire accidental. In retrospect, it seemed as if she'd been gauging Simon's reaction, checking to see if he'd made the connection between the fire and the death threat.

Was the exquisite, intelligent Nell attempting to protect her father's interests by driving Simon—the earl's favorite—from the house? Or was Oliver attempting to cast suspicion on someone other than himself?

I gazed contemplatively at the man sitting across the table from me. His meek exterior might disguise a veritable snake pit of jealousy and resentment. He might envy Simon's looks, his easy way with people—even his marriage.

"Are you married, Oliver?" I asked.

Oliver turned beet-red and ducked his head just as Giddings arrived with fresh toast. Giddings placed the toast rack at my elbow, examined the serving dishes on the sideboard, and departed.

"You know, Oliver," I said after a moment of silence, "marriage isn't for everyone."

"It is in my family." A note of wistfulness entered his voice. "I simply haven't been lucky enough to find someone as . . . useful . . . as Gina."

It was a revealing comment. Oliver, it seemed, was being subjected to the same kind of pressure Derek had experienced as a young man. Like Derek, he was expected to make a useful match—to place duty before love. Derek had been strong enough to resist the earl's demands, but Oliver seemed more frail.

"I'm not sure usefulness is the first quality I'd look for in a mate," I said gently.

"You would if you were an Elstyn." Oliver paused. A tiny smile lifted the corner of his mouth as he glanced at me. "On second thought, perhaps you wouldn't. You'd marry for love and damn the consequences."

I looked at him closely. "What sort of consequences?"

"Estrangement from one's family." He lowered his eyes. "A questioning of rights that would otherwise be assumed."

"Is that why everyone's here?" I pressed. "Is Derek's birthright in question?"

Oliver lifted his eyes to gaze at me somberly. "I should think so," he said. "I should think it very likely. Uncle's not getting any younger. He's got to consider the future."

"Would it be legal for someone other than Derek to inherit Hailesham?" I asked.

"Gina can find a way to make anything legal," Oliver replied. "She's extremely good at what she does, especially when she has a vested interest." He hesitated. "I imagine you've run into similar difficulties in your family."

I nearly sprayed the tablecloth with tea. After a valiant swallow, I hastened to clear up Oliver's extraordinary misconception.

"My family consisted of my widowed mother and me," I told him. "Our entire apartment could have fit into your uncle's drawing room. I never had to fight for my inheritance because a) there was no one to fight with, and b) there was nothing to inherit. So, no, I've never experienced anything remotely like the difficulties you're describing."

"I do so admire your frankness." Oliver sighed deeply. "The trouble with my family is that no one tells the truth. Claudia says she misses her husband, but she doesn't. Derek and Uncle Edwin act as if they hate each other, but they don't."

"Don't they?" I interjected.

"They wouldn't be able to inflict such dreadful wounds on each other if they didn't love each other." Oliver glanced toward the windows. "Then there's Simon. My perfect brother. Poor chap. He pretends to be happy, but he isn't."

I toyed with my fried tomatoes. "Why isn't Simon happy?"

Oliver laid his knife and fork aside, saying, "I'm hoping you'll find out."

I looked up from my plate, startled.

"Something's troubling Simon," Oliver went on, his brow furrowing. "It's been troubling him for some time. He won't—he can't—admit it to any of us, but I think he might tell you."

I focused on the tomatoes. "What gives you that idea?"

"He likes you," Oliver replied.

"If you ask me," I said, "your brother likes anything in a skimpy dress."

Oliver smiled but shook his head. "I watched the two of you in the rose garden last night. He was looking at you, Lori, not your dress. He trusts you."

"He's only known me for five minutes," I protested.

"Sometimes that's all it takes," Oliver said. "Perhaps it's because you're not part of our world. You're not an Elstyn, you're not English, and you weren't born to wealth." He rested his hands on the arms of his chair. "My brother hasn't met many women like you, Lori. You speak your mind. You don't paint your face or color your hair. You don't try to conceal the fact that you're dazzled by Simon, or irritated by Claudia, or jealous of Gina."

I felt myself go crimson. "Remind me never to play poker with you, Oliver. In fact, remind me never to play poker, period."

"It's nothing to be ashamed of," Oliver said earnestly. "You simply can't help being honest. Perhaps that's why my brother trusts you. I'm convinced that he'll confide in you."

It was comforting to know that although Oliver had discerned much from my treacherously transparent countenance, he hadn't yet figured out that his big brother had already confided in me.

"Oliver," I said slowly, "if you're asking me to spy on Simon—"

"I'm not," he interrupted. "I'm asking you to listen to him, to give him a chance to talk about what's troubling him. I'm asking you to be his friend. He doesn't have any, you see. He has allies and associates, yes, but not a single friend."

"What about his wife?" I asked.

"Oh, no, not Gina." Oliver lowered his eyes. "Gina's a useful ally, not a friend."

I stared down at my plate, but the food had lost its savor. I understood more clearly, now, why Simon was his uncle's favorite. Simon loved Hailesham and horses, and he'd married a woman who was more than capable of managing a large and complex family fortune. Whether she loved him or not seemed—in Oliver's mind, at least—to be an open question. Simon had willingly walked a path Derek had refused to tread. Did he think it would lead to his installation as Lord Elstyn's heir?

I lifted my gaze. "You're Simon's friend, aren't you, Oliver?"

"In my family," he said softly, "brothers aren't permitted to be friends."

"Damn it, Derek!"

Oliver and I jumped, startled by the earl's earsplitting shout.

"My golden girl, in love with an overgrown *stable boy*?" Lord Elstyn's furious roar reverberated from the marble walls of the entrance hall. "I won't hear of it!"

"She seems to be over it, Father." Derek was in the entrance hall, too, and he was making no effort to keep his voice down. "But Emma wanted me to put you in the picture, in case it crops up again. I told her it would be a mistake."

"One of many to be laid at your door," the earl thundered. "I blame you for this unthinkable dalliance. If you hadn't married beneath you, Nell would never have considered—"

"Nell would be lucky to have Kit!" Derek bellowed, matching his father decibel for decibel. "But the fact of the matter is that Kit will have nothing to do with her."

"He won't have *her*?" the earl sputtered. "I've never heard of such insolence. If this Kit Smith sets foot on my property, I'll have him shot."

"Kit wouldn't come here for a king's ransom," Derek retorted. "He's far too decent a chap."

"Sack him!" shouted the earl.

"I have no intention of sacking him," Derek declared stoutly. "Kit's more than an employee. He's a friend. Emma and I depend on him."

"You care more for yourself than for your daughter," the earl scoffed. "I might have known. Gina, Bill, come with me. I have nothing more to say to this . . . this *ingrate*."

Doors slammed and footsteps pounded up the marble staircase. Then all was silence.

Oliver looked shell-shocked. "What on earth . . . ?"

"Nell has a crush on a man who works for Derek," I explained. "It's nobody's fault, and he's not interested. I'm not sure it would be such a bad thing if he were."

Oliver glanced fearfully toward the entrance hall. "My uncle would disagree."

"Your uncle," I said, "hasn't met Kit."

"I hope to God he never does," Oliver said fervently. "Burning bushes are bad enough, but it would be much worse to dodge flying bullets."

I thought of the poison-pen letter and hoped Oliver's words wouldn't prove to be prophetic.

Nine

Oliver went to his room to make phone calls and, I suspected, to reduce the chances of running into his irate uncle. I was on my last cup of tea when Giddings returned to the dining room bearing a brown-paper-wrapped parcel addressed to me. I recognized the handwriting on the label, gave the package an exploratory squeeze, and smiled.

"It's from my children's nanny," I told Giddings. "She must have noticed that I forgot to pack my dress shoes and sent them along to me."

"Would you like me to place the item in your room, madam?" Giddings inquired.

"Yes, please," I said, glancing at my watch. "Would you also direct me to the library? I'm told it's very beautiful."

"The library is on the ground floor of the central block, madam, two doors up from the drawing room." Giddings bowed. "I will escort you, if you wish."

"No, thanks," I said. "I'm sure you have more important things to do."

"As you wish, madam." Giddings took the parcel from me and left the room.

I waited for five minutes, checked to see if the coast was clear, and darted across the entrance hall, thanking

Aunt Dimity once again for her sartorial assistance: The soft-soled flats she'd advised me to wear didn't make a sound on the marble floor.

I opened the door to the library at precisely nine o'clock. It was a spacious, rectangular room with a coved ceiling. The west-facing windows were shrouded in dark green velvet drapes, to guard the leather bindings from the ravages of the afternoon sun. The walls were hung with leaf-green watered silk, and a pair of enormous Turkish carpets covered the parquet floor. The mahogany bookcases rested on finely carved bases and were enclosed by diamond-paned glass doors.

An assortment of reading chairs, library tables, display cabinets, and map cases had been tastefully arranged to form bays in which the studious could go about their business without disturbing others. I expected to find Simon lurking in the bay farthest from the door, but the person I found seated at the table there seemed to be as surprised to see me as I was to see him.

"Who are you?" he blurted.

He was a young man with Asian features, an uncombed thatch of jet-black hair, and oversized wire-rimmed glasses that were at least twenty years past their fashion sell-by date. His blue jeans were faded and his white shirt, though spotless, looked as if it hadn't felt the touch of an iron in months. I was fairly certain he wasn't an Elstyn.

"I'm Lori Shepherd, one of Lord Elstyn's houseguests," I replied. "Who are you?"

The young man pushed his chair back from the table and got to his feet. He was as tall as Simon but as thin as a rail, and he stood with his shoulders hunched forward, as if he were self-conscious about his height.

"I'm, um, Jim Huang." His eyes darted nervously from me to the door, as if he were planning an escape route.

I glanced down at the table. A manuscript box and a small reading lamp sat at one end, a laptop computer at the other. Between them lay a magnifying glass and neatly stacked piles of loose papers that appeared to be letters. They looked nothing like the one Simon had received. These were written in a feminine hand on fussy stationery.

"Nice to meet you, Jim," I said, hoping to put the young man at ease. "You sound as if you're from the States."

"I'm from Kalamazoo, Michigan," he admitted.

"Chicago," I said cheerfully, pointing to myself. "I'd say that makes us neighbors. What are you doing so far from home?"

"I'm an archivist." Jim switched off the reading lamp and began methodically to gather the notes and return them to the manuscript box. "Lord Elstyn hired me to sort through some family papers."

"Don't let me chase you away," I urged.

"It's okay," he said, closing the laptop. "I was about to take a break anyway."

Jim's twitchiness and the speed with which he'd cleared the decks suggested to me that he was working on yet another of the earl's highly confidential projects. I wasn't interested in what he was doing, but I did want to pick his brain about a few other matters.

"Been here long?" I asked.

"Ten days," he replied.

I turned to survey the room. "It's a lovely place to work. I'll bet people are in and out of here all the time."

"You're the first, apart from the earl." Jim pushed his oversized glasses up his nose and gazed about the room. "It's surprising, really, because the collection's *amazing.*"

I recognized the note of enthusiasm in his voice because I'd heard it so often while working in my alma mater's library. Unless I was very much mistaken, Jim Huang was a born bibliophile. I felt as if he'd given me a gift.

"Amazing, huh?" I said. "I don't suppose you'd have the time to show me a few of the highlights."

"Well . . ." He glanced anxiously at the door.

"I won't tell the earl, if that's what's worrying you," I assured him. "It's just that I don't know much about books. It'd be great to learn about them from someone who really knows his stuff."

The dumb-little-me routine worked like a charm. In no time at all Jim had forgotten about his break and begun a guided tour of the shelves.

Ardor loosened his tongue and he talked a mile a minute as he walked, describing early editions of works by Austen, Defoe, and Fielding. He was extremely knowledgeable about classic English literature, but his greatest joy seemed to come simply from handling the books. I understood the sensation. There were few things in life as satisfying as the pebbly texture of a fine morocco binding or the chance discovery of an author's inscription. Jim Huang seemed to have thumbed through every volume in the room.

"It sounds as if you've been camping out in here," I commented when we reached the end of the tour.

"No such luck." Jim returned a first edition of Christopher Smart's *Hymns for the Amusement of Children* to the shelf, aligned it precisely with the other volumes, and closed the glass doors. "I sleep in the servants' quarters. It's not as bad as it sounds. Lord Elstyn treats his hired help really well."

"So if I came in here during the night," I said, "I wouldn't run the risk of tripping over you?"

"Not me." Jim laughed. "You might trip over the earl, though. He's in here most nights, reading. I think he's an insomniac." His smile vanished suddenly, as if by mentioning the earl he'd reminded himself of the work he was neglecting. "Look, I'm sorry, but I have to go."

"I understand," I told him. "Thanks for showing me around. I learned a lot."

Jim returned to the table to pick up the laptop and the manuscript box, then paused on his way out.

"If you're looking for something great to read," he said, "I stand ready to help. Giddings always knows where to find me." He nodded to me in a friendly fashion and left the room, his precious project cradled in his arms.

I glanced at my watch. It was nearly ten o'clock and there was still no sign of Simon. I considered searching for him but decided to stay put. There was no point in both of us running in circles and a library was one of my favorite places to kill time.

I was perusing an 1814 Military Library edition of *Mansfield Park* when the door opened and Simon appeared. Though slightly out of breath, he still managed to look elegant in a black cashmere sweater tucked into pleated charcoal-gray trousers.

"I'm so sorry, Lori," he said, closing the door behind him. "My new hunter tossed me into a muddy morass and the cleanup took longer than I'd anticipated."

"Don't worry about it," I said. "I've made good use of my time."

"You intrigue me." Simon crossed the room and lowered himself gingerly into the leather armchair opposite mine.

"Are you hurt?" I asked, wondering how far the new horse had tossed him.

"I'm fine," he replied. "Tell me what you've been up to in my absence."

I laid *Mansfield Park* aside and sat forward in my chair. "You asked me here to help you find the books that were chopped up by whoever created the poison-pen letter, right?"

"I don't need to explain much to you, do I?" he said, smiling.

"It was a logical assumption." I gave silent credit to Aunt Dimity, then went on. "I think I've saved us a lot of wasted effort. Have you met Jim Huang?"

Simon looked blank. "Jim . . . ?"

"Huang," I said. "He's working on a project for your uncle. He knows this collection like the back of his hand and he's slightly unhinged when it comes to keeping the books in order. He'd notice if anything was damaged, missing, or out of place."

"Has he noticed any such thing?" Simon asked.

"Nope." I rested my elbows on my knees. "Jim also told me that the library's almost always in use, either by him or by your uncle."

"Which would make unobserved access difficult." Simon steepled his fingers. "If Mr. Huang's as protective of the books as you seem to think, I doubt that he'd cut them up, and I refuse to suspect my uncle of threatening me or burning the turtledove. Who else has been in the library and when?"

"I don't think it matters, because there's something else. . . ." It was a detail that had been niggling at me ever since Dimity had mentioned the odd typeface that had helped her catch *her* poison pen. "Did you bring the note with you?"

Simon clenched his jaw as he leaned forward to pull the folded sheet from his back pocket. The movement seemed to cause him such discomfort that I scooted over and knelt beside his chair, to save him the trouble of handing the note across to me. I took the folded sheet, spread it flat on the arm of his chair, and felt a small rush of elation.

"Look," I said, pointing to each individual letter. "The letters aren't just different sizes, they're different colors as well. And the fonts aren't standard fonts, they're . . . whimsical."

"A whimsical death threat," Simon noted dryly. "There's an original idea."

"My point is," I said eagerly, "whoever pasted together your death threat used *children's* books. We shouldn't be down here at all. We should be in—"

"The nursery," Simon whispered, "where no one ever goes." His blue eyes glowed with admiration. "Lori, you are brilliant. I'd never have thought of the nursery on my own. How can I ever repay you?"

"By telling me the truth." I gazed at him steadily and pointed to the death threat. "Is this the first poison-pen letter you've received?"

Simon lifted an eyebrow. "Why do you ask?"

"It's something Oliver said," I replied. "He told me that something's been troubling you *for some time*."

"Oliver said that?" Simon seemed surprised.

"He's an observant sort of guy," I said, "and he's worried about you, so it occurred to me that—"

Giddings chose that moment to make an ill-timed and unwelcome entrance.

"Pardon me, sir, madam." The manservant bowed to Simon. "Lord Elstyn requires your presence in the study, sir."

"Now?" Simon asked.

"Immediately, sir. Lord Elstyn was adamant." Giddings bowed again and departed.

Simon gave an exasperated sigh, refolded the note, and thrust it into my hands. "You go ahead to the nursery, Lori. The north wing, third story, above my room and yours. I'll join you as soon as I can."

He got to his feet so slowly that it was all I could do to keep myself from reaching out to support him.

"Are you sure you're okay?" I asked.

"Never better." He took a shallow breath, squared his shoulders, and went to face his uncle.

"And people wonder why I don't ride horses," I muttered, and set off to find the nursery.

Ten

As I climbed the main staircase, it dawned on me that I might not want all and sundry to see the poison-pen letter Simon had passed into my keeping. My tweed skirt had no pockets, so I tucked the folded sheet into the waistband at the back, where my cardigan would conceal it.

I was straightening my sweater when Emma came running up the stairs, calling my name. She'd exchanged her riding gear for a crimson lambswool sweater and slim black trousers. Her face was ruddy from the morning's equestrian adventure and she seemed in high spirits.

"Have you seen Derek?" she asked when she reached me.

I started to reply but fell silent when a stout, red-haired maid walked briskly across the second-story landing, carrying an armload of towels. I waited until the maid had disappeared into the south wing, then drew Emma over to sit beside me on an embroidered bench on the landing.

"I haven't *seen* Derek." I lowered my voice to keep other prowling servants from overhearing our conversation. "I heard him, though, him and his father, a couple of hours ago, downstairs in the entrance hall. He took your advice, Emma. He told Edwin about Kit and Nell."

Emma kept her own voice low. "How did Edwin take it?"

I rubbed my chin meditatively. "He threatened to shoot Kit, but he didn't say one word about sending Nell to a convent, so on the whole it didn't go too badly."

"*Shoot Kit?*" Emma repeated, her eyes widening in dismay.

"Only if he comes here," I told her. "Which seems unlikely. I know I should've kept track of Derek, but—"

"It's okay," Emma interrupted, and ducked her head. "Derek's right, Lori. I've been far too melodramatic about his homecoming. Now that I've had a chance to meet his cousins, I'm not worried about any of them murdering him in his sleep. If there's fighting to be done, it'll be done with lawyers, not daggers." She touched my arm. "I'm sorry I worried you."

"What are friends for?" I said, and heaved a private sigh of relief. Emma had unwittingly spared me the impossible task of reassuring her without betraying Simon's confidence. "You seem to be settling in."

"I was nervous at dinner last night," Emma admitted, "but Oliver bent over backwards to put me at ease. Edwin's been decent to me, too, though I suspect he's following Nell's instructions rather than his own inclinations."

"Nell must be tickled pink to have you here," I said.

"She is," Emma agreed. "I wish Derek and his father weren't so prickly with each other. Nell would love to invite us here more often."

"Do you think she'd like to live here permanently?" I asked.

"Definitely," said Emma. "Hailesham Park is her natural habitat. She was born to reign here."

"But she doesn't stand a chance of reigning here unless Derek reigns here first," I observed.

"Aye, there's the rub." Emma touched a finger to her wire-rimmed glasses. "I have to admit that, after my ride this morning, I'm prejudiced in favor of Hailesham."

"I take it you had a good time," I said.

Emma's face lit up. "I had a ball, though I was completely outclassed. Claudia's not as silly as she seems, Lori. She rides almost as well as Nell."

"And Simon?" I put in casually.

"Simon's a centaur," Emma said, laughing. "He took a spill on his second go over the hurdles, but that's hardly surprising. It was his first time up on Deacon."

"Is Deacon the dappled gray?" I asked.

Emma nodded. "Simon's new hunter, a gift from Edwin. Deacon's as headstrong as Zephyrus was the first time Kit rode him."

My mind was filled with a sudden, vivid image of Simon sailing gracefully over the hurdles, and I felt a surge of admiration for his horsemanship. Kit had spent more time on the ground than in the saddle when he'd first ridden his black stallion. That Simon had managed the hurdles once on Deacon without incident was more than enough to impress me.

"He must have landed softly, though," I ventured. "The great lawn's pretty muddy, isn't it?"

"It's dry as a bone," Emma countered. "Simon landed like a ton of bricks, but he bounced back up and didn't fall again. He's an experienced rider, Lori. He knows how to fall without hurting himself." She glanced at her watch. "I have to find Derek. I have good news to tell him." She held her hand up to silence me. "I can't tell you until I've told him, and I can't tell him until I've found him."

"Have you been upstairs yet?" I asked.

"I was on my way," said Emma, "when Giddings told me about a carpenter's workshop across from the stables. I thought I'd check there first."

I nodded. "I'll poke around upstairs while you search the workshop."

"Lunch is at one o'clock." Emma rose. "If you find Derek, ask him to meet me in the dining room, will you?"

"I will," I said, but as I made my way up to the third story, I wasn't thinking about Emma's husband.

Simon had explained his late arrival in the library by saying that he'd needed extra time to clean up after he'd fallen into a muddy morass. It was clear to me now that he'd lied and I thought I knew why.

"Stoic men," I grumbled quietly, "can be as headstrong as horses."

The third-story corridor was as plain as piecrust. The walls were whitewashed plaster, the floorboards scrubbed pine, and globe ceiling lamps took the place of wall sconces. The lamps were unlit, but I had no trouble locating the nursery. It was, as Simon had told me it would be, directly above his room and mine.

I exercised a fair degree of caution as I approached the nursery, half hoping to catch the poison pen at work. I turned the doorknob slowly, nudged the door open with my palm, and carefully peered inside. To my great relief, and even greater disappointment, I saw no one. I

slipped into the room and closed the door noiselessly behind me.

I'd entered the day nursery, a combination playroom
and dining room where allegedly privileged children
were expected to live their lives conveniently apart from
adults, save for an ever-present and, one hoped, devoted
nanny. My boys would have loved the day nursery's plen-
tiful playthings but loathed its splendid isolation.

I wondered if Derek had felt the same way as a boy.
The room looked as if nothing had changed since he'd last
played there. A cushioned window seat ran the full length
of the wall in front of me, beneath six casement windows
hung with crisp white curtains. A yellow sailboat lay dis-
carded on the window seat, as if it had been dropped
there in haste and never remembered.

A model train circled the floor before the hearth's
brass fender, set about with tiny houses, shops, and trees.
In one corner of the room, beside a toy cupboard,
loomed a majestic rocking horse. It was coal-black with
dark brown eyes, a wavy mane, a braided tail, and a splendid blue-and-silver saddle. There was no television in
sight.

A wooden table and two chairs sat to one side, as if
they'd been tidied away to make room for the model
train. The wall to my right was covered with a mural de-
picting a young King Arthur brandishing the sword he'd
freed from the stone. To my left I saw a connecting door
beside a large bookcase. Seashells, pinecones, rocks, and
birds' nests cluttered the top shelves, but the lower
shelves were filled with books.

I started toward the books but opened the connecting

door instead, curious to see what lay beyond it. I found myself in an elaborate bathroom. Its floor, walls, and ceiling were covered with tile, and it featured a full-sized bath, a pair of sinks, a step stool, two long counters, a towel cupboard, and an overhead drying rack that could be raised or lowered by means of a chain and pulley. I swung the door partway shut and saw that a pair of hooks had been mounted, one high and one low, on the back.

Another door led from the bathroom to the night nursery, where I found furniture designed to accommodate two people. An adult's bed, a comfy rocking chair and footstool, an oak dresser, and a large wardrobe took up one side of the room, while their pint-sized counterparts occupied the other. A worn and battered gray elephant with large floppy ears rested lopsidedly against the pillow on the smaller bed, as if faithfully awaiting the return of the child who'd once cuddled it.

I was about to give the elephant a reassuring pat when I heard the sound of footsteps in the day nursery. I froze, but my heart took off at a gallop. Had Simon managed to break free from his uncle? Or had someone else entered the room, someone bent on distilling poison from the whimsical children's books?

I nodded to the elephant, turned, and crept silently through the bathroom to the half-shut door leading to the day nursery. Scarcely daring to breathe, I leaned forward to see who had entered the room. I shrank back in disbelief when I saw Derek.

He seemed unaware of my presence. He stood in the center of the room, staring at the bookcase's lower shelves. He'd forsaken formal dress for his familiar blue jeans, work boots, and blue chambray shirt. His salt-and-pepper curls tumbled loosely over his forehead, and the rage that contorted his weathered features chilled me to the bone.

I closed my eyes and willed him to leave, not because he frightened me, but because I loved him and Emma. I didn't want my friends to be connected in any way with the deranged message that was tucked into the waistband of my skirt.

When I looked into the room again, Derek's face had changed. He seemed older, somehow, and filled with weariness. He turned away from the bookcase and walked slowly toward the rocking horse. He stood over it for a moment, then reached out to run his fingers through its wavy mane.

"Hullo, Blackie," he said. "Still placing first in the Derby?" His hand fell back to his side, and his shoulders heaved once in a deep, heart-wrenching sigh.

I could keep still no longer. Derek was one of my dearest friends. I felt like a rat for spying on him.

"Derek?" I said, and stepped out of the bathroom.

He swung around, startled. "Lori? What are you—"

"I'm sorry, I didn't mean to . . . Emma asked me to find you, so I . . ." I crossed the room and put a hand on his arm. "Is there anything I can do?"

Derek looked down at me in silence, then walked to the window seat and picked up the sailboat. He turned it slowly in his hands as he murmured, "Don't ever send your sons to boarding school."

I looked from the sailboat to the rocking horse and wondered how old he'd been when he'd been sent away.

"My mother didn't spend much time at Hailesham," he said, still gazing at the sailboat. "She preferred the London house. Or so I'm told. I was only seven when she died—too young to really know her. That'll never happen with your boys."

He sank onto the window seat and rested the sailboat on his knees. I left the rocking horse behind and sat beside him.

"You've never been away from Will and Rob for more than ten days at a time," he said. "Annelise is an extra pair of hands for you, not a substitute mother for your children."

"Your mother's life was very different from mine," I reminded him.

Derek's jaw tightened. "To say that it's a custom doesn't reconcile me to its evil."

"No," I said, and waited.

"I had Winnie," he said, after a time. "Miss Charlotte Winfield. She was quite young when she came to Hailesham, not much older than Nell is now, though she wasn't half as sophisticated as my daughter."

I smiled inwardly. I'd yet to meet anyone as sophisticated as Nell. "Was she your nanny?"

"Winnie was my everything." Derek blew softly and the boat's white sail fluttered. "We held grand regattas on the pond and took long walks through the woods. She bandaged my knees when I scraped them and washed behind my ears despite my howls. She told me stories about pirates and bandits and ghosts, and she sang me to sleep. She sat beside me at my mother's funeral and held my hand as I stood over my mother's grave."

He laid the sailboat aside. I looked at the seashells, the birds' nests, the pinecones littering the bookshelves and seemed to hear the distant sound of a child's lighthearted chatter twined with a young woman's kindly replies.

"Winnie used to sneak down to the kitchen on Cook's day off to make special treats for me." Derek ran a hand through his graying curls. "Do you remember what we had for pudding last night?"

I'd lived in England long enough to know that "pudding" meant dessert and I recalled exactly what we'd had because I'd described it to Aunt Dimity the night before. "Treacle tart."

"It was Winnie's recipe," said Derek. "Father must have ordered Cook to dig it up. I don't know why. Perhaps he thought it would disarm me." Derek closed his eyes. "When I tasted it, it was as if Winnie were sitting across from me, beaming, because she knew it would give me so much pleasure."

I shifted my gaze to the wooden table and chairs, where a curly-haired boy had once smiled sticky smiles at his beaming, girlish nanny.

Beside me, Derek sighed. "Winnie promised to look after Clumps for me when I went off to prep school."

"Clumps?" I asked.

"My elephant," said Derek. "He was rather like your Reginald, only much the worse for wear. Clumps and I climbed Kilimanjaro together. We fought beside Hannibal in the Alps and crossed the mighty Mississippi. Clumps and I were inseparable until it came time for me to go away to school." His voice grew softer. "But I knew Winnie would look after him. I knew they'd both be waiting for me when I came home again. I had so many things to tell her when I came home, so many things. . . ." Derek stared, unseeing, into the middle distance. "But when I came home, she was gone."

"She . . . died?" I whispered.

"She'd been sacked." Derek's mouth twisted bitterly. "My father had decided that since I would be away at school for most of the year, her services would no longer be required. I never saw or heard from her again. I was eight years old."

I thought of myself at eight, running home after school to my mother, as certain that she would be there as I was of my own name, and tried to imagine the shock of finding her gone—not dead, but alive and beyond my reach. I wondered how many crowds Derek had scanned, looking for Winnie, before he'd finally given up the search. Had I been Derek, I told myself, I'd be searching for her still.

"That's when I understood," Derek said abruptly. "My mother spent the last year of her life in London because my father was a heartless swine. I vowed then and there that I would never be like him."

"You're not," I said fiercely. "The only way you could be *less* like him would be to have a sex-change operation." I would have gone on to enumerate the myriad ways in which Derek *didn't* resemble his father, but he forestalled me with a wholly unexpected snort of laughter.

"I must admit that a sex-change operation never occurred to me." Derek struggled for sobriety, but a second snort forced its way out. "Emma would have been terribly disappointed if it had. Might've been worth it, though, just to see the look on Father's face. I'd've made a formidable viscountess."

"You'd be stunning in a tiara," I agreed, and with that we both gave way to a fit of giggles.

"Poor Blackie," Derek said when he'd regained his composure. "It's been too long since he's heard the sound of laughter."

"Didn't Nell or Peter or Simon's son stay here when they were little?" I asked.

"They've had suites of their own in the south wing since before they could walk," Derek told me. "Father's always been more indulgent with his grandchildren than he was with me."

"It's awfully tidy for a place that's never used." I ran my finger along the windowsill, then held it up for Derek's inspection. "Look. No dust."

"Father would never let something as plebian as dust alight on Hailesham." Derek looked around the room and shook his head. "No, Lori, this place is full of ghosts. You should bring Rob and Will to play here. They'd fill it with life again."

I gave him a sidelong glance. "There's one ghost you might be happy to see."

When he looked at me questioningly, I told him to visit the night nursery. He disappeared through the doorway, but I stayed behind. Some reunions were meant to be private.

He was gone for perhaps ten minutes and when he returned his face was such a cauldron of emotions that I didn't know which one would bubble over first. The elephant he cradled in his arms, however, was already looking less forlorn.

"I'm taking him to Nell," Derek stated firmly, making it

clear that, as a grown man, he could not be expected to display affection for a stuffed animal, however dear.

"I'm sure Bertie will welcome a new companion," I said, thinking of Nell's unabashed devotion to her chocolate-brown teddy.

Derek stroked Clumps's trunk absently. "If you see Emma, will you tell her that I've decided to take lunch in our room? I need to be alone for a while."

"I'll tell her," I said.

"One more thing . . ." Derek's weathered face grew solemn. "Promise me that you won't ever send your children away against their will."

"Derek," I said, "I don't even make my boys eat lima beans against their will."

He smiled and turned to go.

"Derek, wait a minute, will you?" I hesitated, then went on. "You spent the morning with Bill and Gina. Tell me, do they seem to . . . to get along?"

"Hard to say." Derek shifted Clumps to one arm and scratched his head. "They're cordial to each other, but they're both so thoroughly professional that it's difficult to tell what they're thinking, let alone what they're feeling. And I have to confess that I was paying rather more attention to my father than to them." He peered at me intently. "Why? You're not . . . worried about them, are you, Lori?"

"Worried? Me?" I tried to toss off a carefree laugh but couldn't squeeze it past the lump in my throat. I ducked my head. "Maybe I am. A little. They've known each other for a while now, and Gina's awfully attractive."

"Do you think so?" Derek seemed to give the matter

serious consideration. "She's too cold and calculating for my taste, not at all the sort of woman Bill would find attractive." He reached over to raise my chin. "He prefers the warmer sort."

"Maybe he needs a change of climate," I mumbled.

"I doubt it," said Derek. "I doubt it very much."

"Okay." I wiped my nose with the back of my hand. "And if you mention a word of this to Emma, I'll never speak to you again."

"Come here, you ridiculous woman." Derek pulled me to my feet for a reassuring hug, then held me at arm's length. "It's between you and me and Clumps, and Clumps can be trusted implicitly. Coming down?"

"Not yet," I said. "My red nose will give me away."

"Bill's mad about you, Lori. Always has been. Always will be." Derek tapped the tip of my nose. "Red nose and all."

I watched him go, then took a few calming breaths and repeated the words *cordial* and *professional* to myself. The exercise would have been more comforting if Bill had whispered Gina's name the night before in a cordially professional way, but he hadn't. He'd said it pleadingly, as if he'd been longing for her.

I couldn't blame him. He and Gina were both lawyers. They spoke the same language, moved in the same circles, shared a world I neither knew nor cared about. Gina was, as Derek had pointed out, cool and calculating. She'd make a refreshing change of pace from hotheaded, impulsive me. And after the many times I'd strayed, Bill probably felt entitled to enjoy a little fling of his own. It wasn't reasonable of me to expect absolute fidelity from my husband.

I was, however, famously unreasonable.

I shook off the waves of doubt that threatened to engulf me and got to my feet. I had no time to waste on Bill and Gina at the moment, and the poison-pen investigation would have to wait. Derek needed Emma now. I had to head her off before she reached the dining room.

Eleven

Giddings was in the dining room overseeing a pair of uniformed maids who were setting the table for lunch. He guided me to a back door that gave access to the graveled courtyard I'd seen from my bedroom's balcony. The workshops, he told me, occupied the row of low stone buildings opposite the stables.

I could have found the workshops by sound alone. The moment I strode into the courtyard I heard a cacophony of telltale noises: the clank of a blacksmith's hammer, the *tink-tink* of a stonemason's chisel, and the high-pitched whine of a band saw. I also smelled the telltale stink of kerosene.

In an instant I forgot all about Emma and raced toward the pillar of black smoke that rose beyond the last low building. I skidded to a halt at the end of the row and peered furtively around the corner just in time to see Nell toss a cloth bundle onto a bonfire.

Nell had exchanged her riding gear for work clothes similar to Derek's, but her long limbs and natural grace made old jeans and Wellington boots seem the height of fashion. She wore a quilted vest over a cornflower-blue cotton shirt, and her golden curls tumbled loosely beneath a tweed cap. She stood with a pitchfork in one hand. A can of kerosene sat a few yards away, at a safe distance from the roaring fire.

"Hi, Nell," I said, coming up behind her. "We hardly had a chance to say hello last night."

"You were captivated by Simon," she said. "Isn't he lovely?"

"He's, er, very nice," I agreed, and hastily changed the subject. "How's life at the Sorbonne?"

"*C'est merveilleuse*," she replied. "Bertie and I have invited Mama, Papa, and Peter to spend Christmas with us in Paris."

I stared at her, nonplussed. "You're not coming home for Christmas?"

"No," she replied. "I'm afraid the vicar will have to find another Virgin for the village play this year." She stepped forward to poke at the burning cloth with her pitchfork.

"That's quite a blaze you've got going," I commented. "What're you burning?"

"Rubbish," she said.

I gazed at the bundle as the flames consumed it. "Looks like old clothes to me."

"Fleas in the horse blankets," she said serenely. "It happens even in the best-kept stables." She stepped back and rested her pitchfork on the ground. "Did you think it might be old clothes?"

"I . . . didn't know what it was." I cleared my throat. "I was looking for your stepmother when I—"

"Smelled the paraffin." Nell continued to watch the fire. "The stench is unmistakable."

"I noticed it last night," I said, "when the turtledove was burning."

Nell clucked her tongue but didn't seem distressed. "Careless gardener," she murmured. "Careless blacksmith."

"So you think it was an accident?" I asked.

Nell turned to me, her blue eyes wide and innocent. "What else could it be?" She looked back at the fire. "Did Papa find his elephant?"

I blinked stupidly. "How did you know about Clumps?"

"I thought Papa might go up to the nursery," said Nell, "after his meeting with Grandpapa."

"But . . . how did you know that *I* went to the nursery?" I asked.

"A birdie told me." Nell picked up the can of kerosene. "Mama is in the carpenter's shop. If you'll excuse me, I must change for lunch."

Nell shouldered the pitchfork and headed for a collection of white-arched Victorian greenhouses that lay beyond the stables, the source, no doubt, of the earl's delicious peaches—and the storage place for the kerosene.

I would have gone after her, but my mind was in a whirl, a not infrequent result of a conversation with Derek's bewildering daughter.

Why had Nell mentioned "a birdie"? Had she been alluding to the death threat's first line—*Watch the birdie*—and, by inference, to the burning turtledove?

I doubted that Simon had shown the nasty note to Nell, which meant that there were only two ways she could have known its contents. Either the poison pen had shown it to her or she'd pasted it together herself.

Her mention of Clumps made me particularly uneasy. Nell couldn't have known about Derek's floppy elephant unless she'd spent time in the nursery, near the children's books—the likely source of the death threat's whimsical lettering.

Had Nell been taunting me? Was she telling me that she knew who was harassing Simon? Or was she letting me know that she was both poison pen and arsonist and that, try as I might, I'd never prove it?

It wasn't hard to guess how she knew of my alliance with Simon. Oliver had deduced an awful lot from observing his brother and me in the rose garden. Nell would be able to deduce even more. She knew me, knew of my involvement in solving a few modest puzzles that had cropped up in our village. If she'd seen Simon showing the note to me in the rose garden, my subsequent silence on the subject would have told her that I was working with him on the sly.

My head was swimming with conjecture. I wasn't sure what to think, but if Nell had left the pitchfork behind, I'd've used it to fish out the burning bundle and confirm in my own mind that it was flea-ridden horse blankets rather than a set of clothes an arsonist would want to destroy—which, I told myself, could explain why she hadn't left the pitchfork behind. Nell might be enigmatic, but she was nobody's fool.

A gust of noxious smoke chased me back into the shelter of the courtyard, where I paused to shake the gravel from my shoes. As I straightened, I saw Emma standing in the doorway of the workshop nearest me. She was grinning from ear to ear.

"Come here, Lori," she called. "There's someone I want you to meet."

I followed her into a well-appointed carpenter's workshop. The stone building was low-ceilinged but long, and it contained an amazing array of woodworking tools: saws of varying shapes and sizes, drills, planes, clamps, chisels, tins of nails, pots of glue, whatever might be needed to make or repair anything made of wood.

No one was using the tools at the moment. The band saw's whine had ceased and the only person in sight was a wizened old man seated on a Windsor chair near a wood-stove at the rear of the building. His bald head was as brown and mottled as a knob of burled walnut, and he wore a patched carpenter's apron over a moth-eaten wool sweater and a pair of rough brown dungarees.

Emma's eyes were dancing as we approached the old man, but it wasn't until we stood before him that she spoke.

"Ms. Lori Shepherd," she said with great ceremony, "please allow me the pleasure of introducing you to . . . Mr. Derek Harris."

"Y-you're . . . Derek Harris?" I stammered, gaping at the old man. "The *original* Derek Harris?"

"None other," he replied, favoring me with a gap-toothed grin. "Pull up a chair. Emma and I were talking over old times."

"I'll bet you were." I hauled a heavy oak chair closer to his and sat.

"Mr. Harris taught Derek everything he knows," Emma prompted.

"There's some things can't be taught," Mr. Harris allowed. "Derek, as you call him, had a God-given gift for working with wood, but I helped him make use of it, right enough. He tagged along after me like a puppy when he was home from school." The old man pointed a gnarled finger toward the woodstove. "Found him sleeping on the floor there some mornings, wrapped up in a bit of old blanket. Some folk mistook him for my apprentice. Had no idea he was his lordship's son and heir."

While Mr. Harris enjoyed a reminiscent chuckle, I glanced toward the spot on the floor where the young Derek had slept. How he must have rejoiced, I thought, when he'd been mistaken for the old man's apprentice. The process of distancing himself from his father had already begun.

"Mr. Harris still has apprentices," said Emma. "People come from every corner of England to study under him. It's the same in the other workshops."

"It was his lordship's idea," Mr. Harris put in. "Youngsters champ at the bit to get here because they know his lordship'll look after 'em while they're here, same way he looks after me."

"Lord Elstyn's created a kind of college of craftsmanship," Emma explained, "to keep traditional skills from dying out."

"We're dying out, though." Mr. Harris nodded complacently. "Only a few of the old faces left. Saw one the other day I hadn't seen in years. Took me right back. It happens from time to time, the old ones coming back. Derek never came back, though, not after university. Too angry with his father. Never understood it, his lordship being so kind and all, but there you are: fathers and sons."

It was the second time in as many hours that I'd heard an employee praise the earl's kindness. In the library, Jim Huang had made a point of telling me that Lord Elstyn treated his staff well, and Mr. Harris seemed to consider the earl the most generous of men. I found it difficult to reconcile their image of Lord Elstyn with that of the father who'd so heartlessly dismissed his son's nanny.

"What was Derek like as a boy?" I asked.

"Serious," said Mr. Harris. "Didn't say much, but took everything to heart. No mischief from him, not ever." His eyes nearly disappeared in a mass of wrinkles as he smiled at Emma. "Emma here was hoping for more, but there's no tales to be told of young Derek. He was solemn as a preacher, like his son was before you came along, Emma."

Emma nodded. "Peter had a difficult time of it, after his mother died. When I first met him, he was holding the household together while Derek grieved. It was a lot to ask of a ten-year-old boy."

"He got over it, though, thanks to you." Mr. Harris patted Emma's knee. "Saw the change the first time young Peter came to visit, after you'd come into the family. Did my heart good to see the boy bouncing around, driving his granddad mad with mischief. Peter must be closing in on twenty-one by now. Where is the young rascal?"

"New Zealand," said Emma. "Peter's been all over the world, Mr. Harris, climbing volcanoes, studying whales, collecting medicinal plants in the Amazon basin."

"Making up for lost time, I shouldn't doubt," said Mr. Harris.

I tilted my head to one side. "Have you ever left Hailesham, Mr. Harris?"

"Not since the war," he said. "When you find a place you love, you stick there. No sense looking for what you already have." He pulled a pocket watch out of his apron and consulted it. "It's been a pleasure, ladies, but I must be off to my cottage. His lordship won't let me work more than half-days. Says it's too hard on my ticker."

"Mr. Harris," I said, "if you don't mind my asking, how old are you?"

"Not as old as some, but older'n most." The old man grunted as he got to his feet, but his eyes were merry. "I'm aiming for a century."

Emma and I accompanied Mr. Harris through the workshop's back door, where he climbed into a golf cart and drove toward the woods, waving.

Emma was beside herself with delight and chattered happily as we made our way back to the house.

"Can you believe it, Lori? The original Derek Harris. And Derek—my Derek—doesn't know he's here. I'm not going to tell him, either. I'm going to bring him to the workshop and stand back. I don't know if I can wait until tomorrow morning to see his face. He'll be so *pleased*."

"Is Mr. Harris the good news you wanted to tell Derek?" I asked.

"What?" Emma looked at me blankly, then shook her head. "No, that's something else entirely, though Derek will be glad to hear it. Did you manage to find him?"

I told her that Derek was waiting for her in their room and watched her fly upstairs to meet him. I thought it best to keep my concerns about Nell to myself until I had something concrete to offer. At the moment I had nothing but suspicion.

I wanted to return to the nursery, to examine the children's books, but a glance at my watch told me that lunch would be served shortly, so I headed for the dining room instead. I opened the door and stopped dead on the threshold, astounded to see Bill there, on his own.

My husband stood with his arms folded, gazing out of the window. He was the only person I'd seen so far, apart from Giddings, who hadn't dressed down for the day. Bill's three-piece black suit and crisp white shirt reminded me that our visit to Hailesham Park was, for him, a working holiday.

I gazed at him in silence, admiring the snug fit of his waistcoat, the soft drape of his trousers, the pleasing contrast of the white shirt against his tanned skin. I could tell by the way he held his shoulders, though, that something was amiss, and when he finally turned around, I wasn't surprised to see that his face was as stormy as a March morning.

"Oh, it's you, Lori." His eyes slid away from mine. "Sorry I've been so busy. You must be bored out of your skull."

"Bored?" If there was one thing I hadn't been since we'd arrived at Hailesham, it was bored. "No, I've managed to keep myself entertained. Where's Gina?"

"Working." He glanced at his watch. "I should get back."

"You're not staying for lunch?" I asked.

"Not hungry," he replied.

"You've got to eat sometime," I pressed.

"I'm not hungry," he said sharply. He put a hand to his forehead, as though to calm himself. "You don't understand, Lori. Gina and I . . . the past three months . . . I thought it would blow over, but it's only gotten worse."

I steeled myself for a confession I wasn't quite prepared to hear. "What's gotten worse, Bill?"

He hesitated before muttering, "Lord Elstyn."

I blinked. It wasn't the answer I'd expected.

"I wish Derek hadn't told him about Nell and Kit," Bill went on, speaking half to himself. "It's made my job a thousand times more difficult."

"Your *job?*" I echoed. "It's your *job* that's gotten worse?"

"It's become much more . . . complicated." He put his head down and strode past me. "I'll be working late tonight," he said over his shoulder. "Don't wait up for me."

"I won't," I said, but my words were drowned out by Claudia's entrance.

I sank into a chair at the table, too distracted to respond to Claudia's greeting or do more than nod when Oliver and Nell arrived. My first meeting with my husband in nearly twenty-four hours had left me feeling totally befuddled.

I'd never seen Bill in such a perturbed and unsettled state. Everything he'd said was open to interpretation. He'd been on the verge of telling me about the three months he'd spent working with Gina but had switched over at the last minute to expressing vague concerns about Lord Elstyn. Why had he stumbled from one subject to the other? Was he buckling under the pressure of work—or suffering the pangs of a guilty conscience?

"Would Madam care for oysters?"

I emerged from my tangled thoughts to find Giddings standing over me, offering a serving dish filled with shucked oysters on ice. Dimity's etiquette lessons kicked in and I helped myself to the oysters, then made a game attempt to pay attention to the general conversation.

Claudia was holding forth on the irresponsibility of the

gardeners, though she acknowledged the efficiency of their cleanup efforts.

"They've cut away the burnt bits," she observed. "It'll look frightfully gappy until the new shrubs are planted. Such a pity, but what can one expect of students?"

"Students?" I said.

"From the local agricultural college," Oliver clarified. "They maintain the gardens under the supervision of Walter, the head gardener. It's part of a work-study program."

"Like the apprentices in the workshops," I said.

Oliver nodded. "Uncle Edwin established the workshops years ago. He was ahead of his time in wanting to preserve traditional skills. Without them, of course, a place like Hailesham would be impossible to maintain."

Claudia had evidently tired of the topic because she turned to ask Nell's opinion of Simon's new horse.

"Deacon's an angel," Nell replied airily.

"An angel?" Claudia gazed at Nell in disbelief. "It wasn't too terribly angelic of him to refuse the fence this morning."

"Deacon was startled," Nell said. "He needs a strong hand to guide him."

"No one has stronger hands than Simon," Claudia pointed out. "In my opinion, Deacon's a foul-tempered beast. I won't be a bit surprised if Simon sends him back to the sale rooms." She looked at Oliver. "Where is Simon, anyway?"

"I believe he's conferring with Uncle Edwin," said Oliver.

"Simon's in with Gina and Bill?" Claudia tittered. "What an awkward place for him to be."

"What do you mean?" I demanded, more heatedly than was strictly necessary.

Claudia scarcely looked up from her sole à la meunière. "I mean that poor Simon is no match for Gina and Bill when it comes to brain power. They're such clever clogs and they take things so seriously. They're more suited to each other than—"

"The weather's remarkably fine for this time of year," Oliver put in hastily. He was staring at my knife, which had somehow pointed itself in the direction of Claudia's throat.

I relaxed my grip, but it wasn't until I'd worked my way through a small pool of cucumbers in parsley sauce that I could bring myself to inquire politely, "What does your husband do for a living, Claudia?"

"He's a member of Parliament, one of the party's rising young stars," she replied. "Quite a catch for a girl who couldn't pass her O levels. Uncle Edwin was terribly proud of me. One can never have too many MPs in the family."

I caught Oliver's eye and a look of understanding passed between us. Claudia might be an insensitive, indiscreet moron, but, like Simon, she'd proven her usefulness to the family. Between the two of them, they'd brought a top-notch attorney and a rising young member of Parliament into the fold. If the Elstyns had been a corporation, they would have gotten bonuses.

Lemon tarts appeared, we made them vanish, and the meal was over. As I rose to leave, Claudia asked how I planned to spend the afternoon.

"I'm going to check in with my sons' nanny," I told her, "then catch up on some reading."

"How thrilling," she said. "I'm off to visit an old school friend in Westbury. A pity you can't join us. Tea's at four-thirty in the drawing room, if you can bear to tear yourself away from your book."

"*Books,*" I muttered, and headed back upstairs.

Twelve

F stopped in my bedroom and called Annelise on my cell phone, to thank her for sending my shoes and to make sure that peace reigned on the home front. Will and Rob got into the act with a breathless account of a goat that had strayed into our back meadow, and though Annelise assured me that the animal's owner had retrieved it, I had a sneaking suspicion that goats would reappear when it came time for the boys to compose their Christmas wish lists.

I returned the cell phone to my shoulder bag and changed into a pair of soft wool trousers with roomy pockets so I wouldn't have to carry Simon's poison-pen note in my skirt's waistband anymore. I was retying my shoes when I heard the sound of footsteps in the corridor.

I went to my door and listened. The footsteps paused outside my room, then moved on to Simon's. A moment later I heard his door open and close.

Was someone playing post office again?

I slipped into the hallway, tiptoed to Simon's room, and pressed my ear to his door. At first I heard nothing, then, faintly, came a distinct moan, as if someone was in pain. I recognized the voice.

"Simon?" I called. "Are you all right?"

A moment later the door opened and Simon appeared. His face was pale and drawn, and his black sweater was no longer tucked neatly into his gray trousers.

"It's kind of you to look in on me, Lori," he said, "but there's no need."

"Uh-huh," I said doubtfully, eyeing the beads of perspiration on his forehead.

He put a hand on the door frame, as if to steady himself. "I'm indulging in a bit of a lie-down, that's all. It's been a rather taxing morning."

As he turned to go, I grasped the hem of his sweater, lifted it, and gasped. An ugly, misshapen bruise splashed his fair skin, as if he'd been struck in the side with a sledgehammer.

"Dear Lord," I said, aghast. "What have you done to yourself?"

"I landed badly when Deacon tossed me," he confessed. "It'll be all right. I just need to rest."

He pulled his sweater down, took a step into his room, and swayed, as if his legs were about to give way. I came in behind him, closed the door, and helped him to sit on a divan at the foot of his bed.

"You've been in that stupid meeting for nearly four hours," I fumed. "Didn't Gina notice that you weren't your usual bubbly self? Didn't your uncle? As for Bill, I'll give him such a clout—"

"Bill sensed that something was wrong," Simon broke in. "He tried to cut the meeting short, for my sake, but Gina insisted that we carry on, and I didn't object. I didn't want anyone to suspect that I was injured because . . . It's happened again, Lori." He motioned toward his dressing table.

I crossed to the table and saw a half-sheet of white paper that resembled the death threat in every way except for the message:

a pity you didn't land on your head. better luck next time.

"I found it on my pillow when I came up to change out of my riding clothes," Simon explained.

"It must have been pasted together pretty quickly," I said. "Or prepared ahead of time." I pocketed the note and turned to Simon. "Do you think someone tampered with Deacon before you took him out?"

"Horses aren't like cars, Lori. You can't drain their brake fluid." He took a shallow breath and winced. "My persecutor is mocking me. He's every right to. I'm an excellent rider. The fall was embarrassing."

"The fall was painful." I returned to the divan. "It could have been fatal."

"No one dies of bruised ribs," Simon muttered.

"Your ribs may be broken," I insisted. "You could have a punctured lung or . . . or a concussion. If you go to sleep now, you could slip into a coma."

Simon wiped the sweat from his forehead. "I did see stars as I hit the ground."

"That's it. I've heard enough." I took him by the arm. "Come on, we're going to the hospital."

"Don't be stupid," he protested.

I bent down to look him straight in the eye. "You have two choices, old bean. Either I take you to the hospital or you go there in an ambulance. What's it to be?"

He held my gaze briefly, then bowed his head and murmured, "I don't want the others to know."

"Gina's bound to find out when she comes to bed," I said.

Simon sighed impatiently. "Do you see any sign of Gina in this room?"

I looked around and noticed for the first time that there was no connecting door leading to the next room.

"My wife and I haven't shared a bed in years," he said wearily. "Not since our son was born. She'd rather I find my amusement . . . elsewhere."

It was hardly the time to analyze Simon's marriage, but my next question popped out before I could stop it. "Why did you marry her?"

"Someone had to make a good match," Simon snapped. "Derek hadn't, so it was left to me." He grimaced and held a hand to his side but went on with forced nonchalance. "Though if Derek had been available at the time, I've no doubt Gina would have set her sights on him. She's always regretted marrying the wrong Elstyn."

I didn't know what to say, but further discussion was out of the question anyway. Simon's face had gone from pale to ashen.

"Okay," I said briskly, "here's the plan. If anyone asks, I'll tell them we've gone sight-seeing. Where's the nearest hospital?"

"Salisbury," he replied.

"I've been to the cathedral," I told him. "I've climbed the cedar of Lebanon in the cloisters. I'll have no trouble convincing people that we went there to see the sights."

Simon managed a weak chuckle. "I'd give a lot to see you climb the cedar of Lebanon."

"Maybe you will, one day," I said. "But today it's X rays and an MRI for you."

I used the phone on the bedside table to call Giddings, arranged to have the Mercedes brought around to the front entrance, and asked him to tell the earl not to expect us for dinner. Even if we got back in time for the evening meal, I doubted that Simon would feel up to sitting through it.

I helped Simon don a brown suede jacket, stopped in my room to grab my coat and shoulder bag, and kept a close watch on him as we descended the staircase.

"Why did the meeting go on for so long?" I asked.

"Gina gave me an excruciatingly detailed report on Hailesham's debts and assets," he replied, "compared to which an MRI seems like jolly good fun."

The closest I came to seeing Salisbury's sights was a distant view of the cathedral's floodlit spire. The rest of my visit was spent in the hospital, where, after nearly five hours, the doctor on call managed to allay my worst fears: Three of Simon's ribs were badly bruised, but none were broken, and there was no sign of concussion. Dr. Bhupathi prescribed pain pills, recommended bed rest, and absolutely forbade further excursions on Deacon for at least a week.

I picked up some barley soup and cold chicken sandwiches at a café on our way out of Salisbury, so it was nearly nine o'clock by the time we reached Hailesham. Since lights were blazing in the dining room, Simon directed me to a discreet rear entrance and a secondary staircase, where we'd be unlikely to meet anyone.

Our stealthy return was witnessed only by Jim Huang, who was on his way to his room in the servants' quarters, still clinging to his manuscript box and laptop computer. Fortunately, the dark-haired archivist was more concerned with scolding me for leaving *Mansfield Park* on a table in the library than with taking note of Simon's appearance.

Simon was running on empty. He'd refused to take a pain pill on the way back, on the grounds that it might knock him out so thoroughly that I'd have to call for help to haul him from the car. By the time we reached his room, therefore, he was shuffling along as feebly as old Mr. Harris.

I helped him to remove his shoes, his socks, and his sweater, but left the rest of the undressing to him while I politely turned my back and dug the container of soup and a plastic spoon out of the café's takeaway bag. I waited until he'd crawled under the covers to bring the soup to him.

"I've never been less hungry in my life," he stated flatly.

"Eat anyway," I ordered. "You're not supposed to take your medication on an empty stomach."

I coaxed and wheedled and did everything but play the airplane-spoon game with him, and he eventually downed enough soup to satisfy me. I fetched a glass of water from the bathroom, tipped two tablets into my palm, and insisted that he swallow both.

"You remind me of my nanny," he grumbled irritably.

"You remind me of my three-year-olds," I retorted, and gently rearranged his pillows.

"Just my luck," he muttered. "I finally succeed in luring you to my bedroom only to have you turn it into a nursery."

"That's where I'm going next," I said, and settled on the edge of his bed.

He regarded me gravely. "I wish you wouldn't."

"I have to check out the children's books," I reminded him. "Maybe I'll find something that'll lead me to—"

"I wish you wouldn't," he repeated, though his speech was becoming slurred and his eyelids were drooping. "Our prankster's a malicious beast. I don't like the thought of you being up there alone at night, and I'm bloody useless at the moment."

"You'll feel better tomorrow," I soothed.

"Stay with me," he murmured drowsily.

"I'll stay with you until you fall asleep." I smoothed his hair back from his forehead. "Now close your eyes."

The pain pills saved me the trouble of singing a lullaby. Minutes later, Simon was so deeply asleep that he didn't stir when I bent to kiss his brow.

"Thank you," I said, knowing he couldn't hear. "You didn't have to tell me that Bill tried to cut the meeting short. You could have kept it to yourself."

It wasn't difficult to imagine Bill persisting in his protests until he sensed Simon's reluctance to acknowledge weakness. Only then, out of respect for Simon's unspoken wishes, would Bill have let the matter drop.

Simon had, perhaps unwittingly, given me a great gift. He'd reminded me that, while Bill and Gina might have a few superficial things in common, their souls were as different as night and day. Bill could never be attracted to a woman who prattled on about money while her husband sat suffering before her.

Bill had never placed profit above compassion. He'd find it frustrating to work with someone who did. The emotion I'd heard in his voice when he'd whispered Gina's name had more likely been exasperation than longing. I still wasn't sure what had happened between them over the past three months, but I was certain that such a woman could never touch Bill's heart.

"I wish your life were different, Simon," I whispered. "You deserve better than Gina. And when I find out who's tormenting you, I'm going to hang him—or her—out to dry."

Thirteen

F put in an appearance in the drawing room, to make my apologies to Lord Elstyn for missing dinner, but he wasn't there. He hadn't made it to the dining room, either. The earl and his trusty counselors had taken their meal on trays in the study. They were still there.

Nell, too, was absent. When I asked where she was, Derek laughed.

"She's in her room, writing an essay on the lays of Marie de France," he said. "She must be taking her year at the Sorbonne very seriously, to favor Marie de France over me and Emma."

"I don't mind," said Emma, with a meaningful look in my direction. "I'm glad she's absorbed in her schoolwork. It'll keep her from being . . . homesick."

I silently translated "homesick" to mean "lovesick for Kit Smith" and nodded my agreement. The longer Nell stayed away from home, the easier it would be for her to outgrow her infatuation with the Harrises' stable master.

"Simon's worn out, is he?" Claudia queried after hearing my explanation for his absence. "I would be, too, if I'd spent the morning closeted with Uncle Edwin. Uncle's been in a filthy mood ever since he spoke with you, Derek."

"My father's been in a filthy mood ever since—" Derek broke off when Emma touched his arm.

"Where did you and Simon have dinner?" Emma asked, steering the conversation in what she thought was a safer direction.

I hastily pulled up memories of the day Bill and I had spent in Salisbury, before the twins were born.

"The Shuttleworth Inn," I replied, hoping the restaurant still existed. "We needed a solid meal after climbing the stairs up to the spire and hiking around the Roman hill fort at Old Sarum. To tell you the truth, I'm pretty whacked. I think I'll follow Simon's example and turn in early."

"Aren't you going to wait for your husband?" Claudia inquired.

"Bill's working late," I told her.

"Poor lamb," Claudia cooed. "It must be dreadful for him to be locked away with Gina while you and Simon frolic."

"Bill came here to work," I said.

Claudia arched her eyebrows. "Is that *all* he came here to do?"

Both Derek and Oliver caught the sly insinuation in her tone and would have intervened, but I silenced them with a confident smile. Thanks to Simon, I was immune to Claudia's sophomoric baiting.

"Bill works for a living," I said brightly. "It's not a concept I'd expect you to understand, Claudia, but perhaps your husband will explain it to you one day, if he can get a word in edgewise. Good night, all."

I left the room before Claudia had time to collect the few thoughts that were at her disposal and went upstairs. I took a short detour to look in on Simon and was pleased to find him sleeping peacefully. I smoothed his blankets as tenderly as I would have smoothed my sons', grabbed the chicken sandwiches, and headed for the nursery.

The babble of voices in the drawing room grew fainter as I climbed higher and faded entirely when I reached the third-floor corridor. Enough light spilled down the hallway from the staircase for me to find my way to the nursery door, where I stopped to listen.

Was Nell in her room writing an essay? I asked myself. Or was she in the nursery, working on a more dramatic composition? I bent to peer through the keyhole. The room was dark and as silent as a tomb. Simon's malicious beast—whoever he was—had evidently chosen to spend the night elsewhere, so I let myself in, closed the curtains, and lit a wall lamp.

Since Simon and I hadn't enjoyed a bountiful repast at the dear old Shuttleworth Inn, I was hungry enough to chew the paint off the walls. I devoured the slightly soggy chicken sandwiches with gusto, disposed of the wrappers in the café's bag, and only then began my long-delayed search for clues. My first stop was the toy cupboard.

It didn't take long to strike gold. On the third shelf from the top, hidden behind a toy fire engine and a wooden box filled with tin soldiers, I found a stack of white paper, a pot of paste, and an old-fashioned straight razor with an ultrasharp blade—a useful tool for a maniac intent on dissecting books.

The paste was fresh, so I assumed it wasn't a remnant of Derek's prep-school days, and the paper matched the half-sheets in my pocket, but the razor was the biggest prize of all. As I lifted it from the shelf, I saw that its tortoiseshell handle was worn and chipped and inlaid in silver with the Elstyn family crest.

I'd seen the crest on every piece of china in the dinner service. I couldn't be mistaken. The razor had to be a family heirloom, yet here it was, beside the paste and paper, a vital part of the poison pen's handy-dandy toolkit.

The razor seemed to point like an accusing finger at a member of the family, but which one? I contemplated hiding in the bathroom to lie in wait for the culprit but vetoed the plan as impractical. Bill would sound the alarm if he found my bed empty in the middle of the night or ask the kind of questions I couldn't answer without betraying Simon's confidence.

After a moment's thought, I slipped the razor into my pocket with the two nasty notes. I'd show it to Simon first thing in the morning, let him draw the obvious conclusions, and follow the trail wherever it might lead.

Heartened by what I considered to be a sensational discovery, I crossed the room, sat cross-legged on the floor, and scanned the bookcase's lower shelves. The books were as dated as the nursery itself, as if Lord Elstyn had read them as a child and passed them on to Derek in the fullness of time. The first title to catch my eye was one that would be familiar only to someone who, like me, had worked with obscure volumes.

"Edith Ann!" I exclaimed, delighted.

I felt as if I'd encountered an old friend. Edith Ann Malson's works had been out of print—and out of favor—for more than half a century, thanks to a slightly gruesome sense of humor that went down well with children but gave squeamish parents nightmares. A complete series of Malson's Romney Rat stories was worth a small fortune, and every title was present on Derek's shelves. I could hardly wait to leaf through them but decided to be methodical and started with the first book on the topmost shelf.

For nearly two hours, I paged carefully through fairy tales, folktales, morality tales, Arthurian romances, nature guides, and simplified histories extolling the virtues of the British Empire. By the time I reached Edith Ann Malson's books, I was cross-eyed with fatigue.

I opened *Romney's Rambles,* the first book in the series, turned to the title page, and bolted upright, gasping in dismay. Every colorful capital letter had been excised— the *E, A,* and *M,* along with both *R*'s. Wide-awake now, I leafed through the rest of the book and found that words and letters had been harvested from nearly every page.

My hands were trembling by the time I closed the book, and my sense of outrage was greater even than Jim Huang's when he'd found the unshelved copy of *Mansfield Park.* To some, *Romney's Rambles* might be nothing more than an out-of-date waste of paper, but to me it was a rare and beautiful artifact. Its desecration made me see red.

I took a few slow breaths to steady myself before opening *Romney Returns.* The second volume in Malson's series wasn't as badly mangled as the first, but letters were missing throughout—too many letters, I realized with a start, to account for the two notes Simon had shown me.

I took the notes out of my pocket and placed them side by side on the floor.

The first referred to the fire:

**watch the birdie.
it could happen to you.
Leave hailesham or it will.**

The second concerned Simon's fall from Deacon:

**a pity you didn't land on your head.
better luck next time.**

The poison pen had used a total of ninety-nine individual characters to patch together both messages, yet more than one hundred were missing from the first two Romney Rat books alone. Stranger still, neither message contained the capital letters sliced from the first volume's title page: *E, A, M,* or *R.*

Had the malicious beast set letters aside, to use in future notes? Or had Simon received threats he hadn't yet shared with me?

With grim determination, I opened the third volume in the series, *Romney to the Rescue,* and began counting. I'd just reached the part where Romney saves Monmouth Mouse from a voracious terrier when I caught sight of something that sent a shiver down my spine.

There, curled on the page, in the blank space beneath the illustration, lay a single strand of hair that gleamed like liquid gold. I knew of only one person whose hair seemed to give off light even on the cloudiest of days. She was in her room, writing an essay on Marie de France.

"Nell," I whispered. "Nell, how *could* you?"

A host of vivid images flashed through my mind: Nell on the staircase, gazing intently at Simon; Nell throwing the cloth bundle onto the bonfire; Nell calling Deacon *an angel* . . . and my heart sank. There was a fine line between madness and eccentricity. Nell, spurred by the desire to protect her father, had clearly crossed it.

I laid the golden strand atop the poison-pen notes, folded the notes together, and put them in my pocket with the straight razor. I reshelved the books, turned off the light, and left the nursery. I didn't feel angry anymore. I felt sick.

Not a sound rose from the drawing room as I descended the staircase. The others had evidently gone to bed. I peered in at Simon and saw that he was still soundly asleep. I checked Bill's room, too, but he was nowhere in sight, so I trudged disconsolately to my own room and got ready for bed.

It wasn't until I turned on the bedside lamp that I found the long-stemmed red rose lying on the mound of pillows atop a note written in Bill's familiar hand:

I'm sorry I was brusque with you this afternoon, love.
When this blasted business is over, I'll make it up to you,
I promise.

I felt tears sting my eyes even as I smiled. It seemed ludicrous, now, to think that my greathearted husband could even contemplate a fling with someone as heartless as Gina. Derek had been right. Bill preferred the warmer sort.

Bill's note was music to my ears, but my mind was still in turmoil. I had no idea how to confront Nell or break the news to Derek that his darling daughter was desperately in need of therapy. I pulled Reginald into my arms for comfort, then reached for the blue journal.

Fourteen

Dimity?" I said. "You busy?"

A sense of calm washed over me when Dimity's old-fashioned copperplate began to curl across the page.

I'm never too busy for you, my dear, though you must have had an exceedingly busy day, to end it at such a late hour. I presume the hunt for the poison pen proceeds apace? Tell me all about it.

I looked at Reginald and raised my eyebrows, wondering where to begin. After weeding out Jim Huang, the original Derek Harris, his namesake's banished nanny, Emma's good news—about which I still knew nothing— and a number of other extraneous matters, I was still left with a huge stack of material to cover. I decided to start boldly at the end and work my way backward.

"It's Nell," I declared. "Nell's the poison pen. She's trying to keep Simon from replacing Derek as Lord Elstyn's heir."

The pause that followed was so prolonged that I started to wonder if Dimity had run out of ink. Finally, her response appeared, written crisply, without hesitation.

Was it a sunny day, my dear? Did you stay outside too long without your hat? Have you, in short, PARBOILED YOUR

BRAIN? I've known you to leap to preposterous conclusions before, Lori, but you've outdone yourself this time. Nell would never stoop to threatening someone in such a mean and despicable manner. She's far too self-possessed.

"She wasn't very self-possessed when she sent those love letters to Kit," I pointed out.

Irrelevant. I've never known a woman to be entirely rational when in the early stages of first love, and Nell's long since regained her composure.

I shook my head sadly. "Sorry, but I think she's lost it again."

Then there's the small matter of primogeniture. The inheritance laws in this country are extremely strict. It would be no small matter for Simon to take Derek's place.

"Oliver thinks the fix is in," I said. "Don't forget, Dimity, Derek changed his name and stayed away for twenty years. Oliver thinks a good lawyer could make a case for disinheritance, and Gina's not only a good lawyer, she's married to Simon. She has a vested interest in showing Derek the door."

But Nell has no need to resort to such underhanded methods. Edwin has indulged her every whim ever since she was old enough to have whims. If Nell wished to influence her grandfather, she need only speak to him.

"Simon's been around longer than Nell," I said bluntly. "Besides, he's a man—a married man with a son. He's ready to step up to the plate here and now. I can understand why Nell sees him as a threat."

Conjecture isn't proof, my dear. Can you offer evidence to support your far-fetched accusation?

I leaned back against the mound of pillows and spelled

out my chain of reasoning, for my own benefit as much as Dimity's.

I reminded Dimity that Nell had been late for dinner on the night of the fire and that she'd stared directly at Simon when the fire was mentioned. I told her about the bonfire, the cloth bundle, and the can of kerosene. I explained why Nell's reference to a "birdie" suggested familiarity with the first of the poison-pen notes.

I recounted how the death threat's unusual lettering had led me to the children's books in the nursery and asserted that Nell's allusion to Derek's elephant proved that she'd been there before me.

I described Simon's accident, the second poison-pen note, and Nell's warm praise for the horse that had caused Simon such grievous bodily harm.

I told Dimity about my discovery of the pot of paste, the paper, the vandalized books, and the straight razor with the Elstyn family crest.

Finally, I took the curling strand of golden hair from the folded notes and held it in the lamplight, marveling at its luster—and told Dimity where I'd found it.

Dimity promptly dismantled my chain of reasoning, link by rusty link.

Your evidence is entirely circumstantial, Lori. If enigmatic comments were considered criminal, Nell would have been locked up the moment she learned to speak. I'd be more suspicious if she started babbling inanely about pop music.

"Maybe so," I allowed, "but you have to admit that the bonfire's pretty fishy."

I have to admit no such thing. It's only natural that Nell would know where the paraffin is stored—Hailesham's her sec-

ond home. Have you asked anyone in the stable if the horse blankets were flea-ridden, as she claimed?

"Uh, no," I replied weakly. It had never occurred to me to corroborate Nell's story.

I suggest you do. I also suggest that you learn more about horses before you question Nell's opinion of them. If she considers Deacon good-natured, I have no doubt that he is. I'm afraid we must blame Simon's accident on Simon rather than his horse.

"But what about the razor, the hair?" I demanded.

Although the razor undoubtedly belongs to a member of the family, its owner doesn't necessarily have anything to do with the poison pen. The razor might have been lost, stolen, or borrowed at any time. As for the hair, Nell might have played in the nursery when she was a small child. She might have read the books and discovered Derek's elephant long ago.

"Derek told me that neither Nell nor Peter ever used his old nursery," I said.

Since Derek never visited Hailesham with his children, I doubt very much that he knows where they went while they were here.

Though daunted by Dimity's assault, I was too stubborn to give in to mere logic and made a final attempt to shore up what was left of my flawless argument.

"Don't get me wrong, Dimity," I said. "I don't think Nell's evil. I think she's mixed up. I mean, she's stuck between two worlds. On the one hand, there's her grandfather, who expects her to make a power marriage. On the other hand, there's her father, who'd rather she marry Kit for love than anyone else for money. It doesn't get more opposite than that. She can't help being confused."

Nell inspires confusion in others, Lori. She does not experience it herself.

"Maybe she thinks she can have it both ways," I continued doggedly. "If she frightens Simon off, Derek's place will be assured and one day Hailesham will be ruled by a kinder, gentler earl. When that day comes, she'll be able to live here *and* marry for love."

You're treading water, Lori. You know as well as I do that Nell will do exactly as she pleases, regardless of Edwin's demands. The handwriting stopped for a moment, as if Dimity were reviewing the facts, then resumed. *Your entire argument rests on the assumption that the poison pen hates Simon.*

"Well . . . yeah," I said, taken aback. "Those notes aren't what I'd call fan mail."

Imagine, if you will, that the poison pen loves Simon. Imagine that it's someone who sees the pitfalls of being Lord Elstyn's heir and wants to protect Simon from them.

"There are pitfalls?" I said doubtfully.

The estate is extremely costly to maintain. If the family's finances are in disarray,

I cut her off. "It's not about money. Gina's too smart to saddle her husband with a white elephant, and Simon would take Hailesham under any conditions. I told you, Dimity, he loves the place—and he's rich as Croesus." I stroked Reginald's soft ears and gazed into the middle distance, struck by a new line of reasoning. "Oliver . . ."

Oliver?

"Give me a minute," I said, and tried to remember the wistful words Oliver had uttered during breakfast. "Oliver loves his brother, but I don't think he knows how to express his love. He told me that he and Simon weren't permitted to be friends."

I'm sorry to say that Edwin encouraged competition between them, in a misguided attempt to prepare them for the competitive worlds of school and university.

"Oliver seems to feel sorry for Simon," I said. "When we spoke this morning, he described Simon as his perfect brother, then called him a poor chap, as if being perfect were some sort of burden."

It's an intolerable burden to place on any human being. A perfect man can't ask for his family's help when he's being tormented. He must pretend that all is well, even when he's suffered a grave injury.

"Oliver said that Simon pretends to be happy," I went on, "and that he has no friends, only . . . associates and allies."

Simon has a wife. Isn't she his friend?

My lips tightened into a thin line. "I asked the same question, Dimity, and Oliver told me that Gina isn't Simon's friend—she's a useful ally."

Oh, dear. Poor Simon, indeed, if his attempts to live up to his uncle's standards of perfection have trapped him in a loveless marriage.

"Maybe Oliver's trying to help him find a way out," I offered. "I don't think Gina would be too pleased with Simon if he went AWOL from the summit meeting. It might cause a rift between them, especially if Gina married Simon in order to get her hands on Hailesham."

In other words, Oliver might be harassing Simon in an attempt to free him from an unhappy marriage.

I nodded. "You said that Oliver spent his holidays here as a child. He'd know where the kerosene is stored."

He'd also have access to the straight razor, the nursery, the topiary, and Simon's bedroom. He'd be familiar with the back staircases and side doors.

"Oliver arrived at Hailesham before the others," I said. "He would've had ample time to leave the note in Simon's room and set the fire. He didn't go riding, either, and he went upstairs after breakfast. He could have made the second note and delivered it to Simon's room before Simon got back from the stables."

Oliver seems worth a closer look. I suspect the straight razor will prove to be a useful starting point for the next phase of your inquiry, though I wish you hadn't removed it from the nursery.

"Why not?" I asked.

Its absence is certain to alarm the poison pen. I fear that he may decide to embark upon a more direct campaign against Simon—or you.

"Oliver's trying to help his brother," I protested. "He wouldn't hurt anyone."

You're getting ahead of yourself again, Lori. We don't know that Oliver's the culprit, and until we do, we must assume that someone in this house is quite mad and possibly dangerous. Sleep well, my dear.

My flesh crept as Dimity's handwriting faded from the page, and when I considered the many uses to which the straight razor could be put, I was rather glad I'd removed it from the nursery.

"Lucky me, eh, Reg?" I placed the journal on the bedside table and switched off the lamp. "I wanted to see behind the scenes at Hailesham and I've certainly gotten an eyeful."

I no longer had any difficulty understanding why Derek had rebelled against his family. Their life of privilege came at too high a price. Claudia had been handed every advantage, yet she was as shallow as a birdbath. Oliver's finer feelings had been so thoroughly bludgeoned in childhood that he couldn't admit to loving his own brother. Simon seemed to me to be the saddest of the three, standing alone and lonely atop a precarious pedestal of perfection.

By breaking every one of his father's rules, Derek had found the best kind of happiness. He made a living doing work he loved to do. He adored his wife and children, and they, in turn, adored him. His rambling, imperfect manor house radiated an air of quiet contentment that reflected his hard-won peace of mind.

Perhaps, I thought, it was just as well that Lord Elstyn had fired his son's nanny. Derek's heartbreak had led him to reject things that weren't worth having—and to find things that were.

By the time Bill crawled into bed with me, I was much too sleepyheaded to talk, but we found other pleasant ways to pass the time.

Fifteen

ill was gone when I woke up, but I woke up smiling. Reality, I thought, could sometimes be sweeter by far than the sweetest dreams. I rolled onto my side and gazed lovingly at the sunlight streaming through the balcony door. For the first time since we'd arrived at Hailesham Park, I felt as if I were truly on holiday.

Then I remembered the straight razor and shot out of bed.

I showered in record time and dressed in the loose trousers I'd worn the day before, paired with a claret-colored silk blouse. I gave my damp curls a hasty comb-through with my fingers, tucked the poison-pen items into my pocket, and trotted next door to present the razor for Simon's inspection.

My knock was answered by the heavyset redheaded maid, who set aside her feather duster long enough to inform me that Mr. Simon had gone down to breakfast a half-hour earlier. I thanked her and started down after him. Since I couldn't very well brandish the straight razor over platefuls of kippers and sausages, I'd have to pull Simon aside for a private tête-à-tête after breakfast—unless his uncle nabbed him first.

Claudia, Oliver, Emma, and Derek greeted me as I entered the dining room. I returned their good mornings and did my best to disguise the frustration that welled up in me when I noted Simon's absence.

"Is Simon in with the earl again?" I asked as I loaded up my plate from the sideboard.

"Simon's gone riding," said Claudia.

I dropped a serving fork. Oliver kindly retrieved it and handed it to Giddings, who carried it decorously from the room.

"Porridge this morning!" Derek proclaimed. He seemed remarkably chipper. "I'd forgotten how much I love porridge. You should give it a try, Lori. It's drizzled with honey and swimming with sultanas."

"Did you say that Simon's gone riding?" I said, staring at Claudia in disbelief.

She pointed toward the windows. "See for yourself."

I set my plate on the table and crossed to stand before the windows. My jaw tightened when I saw the dappled gray canter into view, straddled by a long-legged figure in a black velvet helmet, tall black boots, fawn breeches, and a black riding coat.

I simply couldn't believe that Simon would be so stupid, that he would fly in the face of Dr. Bhupathi's expressed orders and endanger his health just to maintain the myth of his invincibility. If he'd been within arm's reach, I'd have slapped him silly.

Claudia followed me to the windows. "He's magnificent, isn't he? Emma, quick—Simon's going to take Deacon over the hurdles again."

"Good for him." Emma joined us, with Derek trailing in her wake. "It's the best thing to do after you've been thrown from a horse. Get right back up and . . ." She frowned suddenly and leaned forward, squinting. "Wait a minute. That isn't—"

"What's going on?" Simon asked from the doorway.

Every head turned in his direction, then swiveled back to watch the dappled gray as it thundered across the turf. Horse and rider were within three strides of the first jump when Deacon came to a jarring halt, veered to the left, and reared wildly, pawing the air with his hooves. The rider clung to his back for a split second, then flew from the saddle in a wide arc and landed hard on the ground. She didn't get up.

For a breathless moment we stood frozen in horror. Then Derek cried: *"Nell!"*

The spell was broken. Derek and Emma raced from the room while Oliver used his mobile phone to call for an ambulance. Claudia disappeared briefly only to reappear tearing down the graveled drive after Derek and Emma, carrying a first-aid kit and an armload of blankets. Simon would have followed if I hadn't seized his arm.

"Go and tell your uncle what's happened," I said, knowing he was in no shape to run. "I think he's in the study."

"Right." He glanced anxiously at the windows, then took off for the study.

"The ambulance is on its way," Oliver announced. "Let's go, Lori."

The next twenty minutes became a sequence of still images: Nell sprawled motionless on the ground, her left arm twisted above her head at an unnatural angle; Derek kneeling helplessly beside her; Emma's hand gripping his shoulder; Oliver on the watch for the ambulance; the earl, looking suddenly old and frail, propped between Simon and Gina.

Bill and I clung to each other and prayed every parent's prayer: *Please let this child live, please don't take her from us, please, please, please. . . .*

Claudia loosened Nell's cravat, spread the blankets over her, took her pulse, lifted her eyelids to peer at her pupils, and spoke to her quite sharply, commanding her to wake up. A siren's nerve-shredding wail had just caught at the edge of my hearing when Nell's lips moved.

"Papa?"

"I'm here, dearest." Derek bent to kiss her brow. "Don't try to move, my darling. Help is on the way."

Oliver waved the ambulance over and we stood back while the medical team went to work. When Bill volunteered to go to the hospital, to slay any and all red-tape dragons that might dare to cross Nell's path, I urged him on without a moment's thought. Bill and I would walk through fire for Derek's children and we knew that he would do the same for ours.

Derek and Emma rode in the ambulance with Nell, and Bill took the Mercedes while Gina and Simon guided the earl into his chauffeured limousine and accompanied him to the hospital. When they'd gone, Claudia went in search of Deacon, and I helped Oliver carry the first-aid kit and the blankets into the house. I dropped the blankets on the entrance hall's polished floor, placed the first-aid kit in one of the marble niches, sat on the stairs, and burst into tears.

Oliver, who looked close to tears himself, instantly came to sit beside me.

"Try not to worry," he said worriedly. "Nell may look delicate, but she's tough as old boots. I sometimes think she's stronger than the rest of us combined. I'm sure she'll be all right."

A petite, gray-haired maid appeared and began to fold the blankets I'd dumped on the floor. My histrionics must have alarmed her because she broke the servants' sacred vow of silence and asked if something was amiss. I stared at her, wondering how on earth she'd missed all of the commotion, but Oliver was patience itself.

"Miss Harris was thrown from her horse," he explained. "She's been taken to hospital."

"Miss Harris was thrown?" said the maid. "How dreadful." She thought for a moment, then added, "I'll light a candle for her, sir."

Oliver thanked her, pulled a white handkerchief from his pocket, and handed it to me. "Why don't you call home, Lori?" he suggested. "It might help to hear your sons' voices."

"My boys . . ." I took a few hiccuping breaths, blew my nose, and wiped my eyes. "That's a great idea. Will you be okay on your own?"

He nodded. "I'll stay by the phone and report to you if I hear anything."

I squeezed his hand gratefully. "I envy the girl who marries you, Oliver. If you ever come to visit me and Bill, I'll introduce you to our nanny. You and Annelise both have hearts of gold."

Oliver colored to his roots but managed a shy smile. "I may take you up on that. A nanny in the family would be very useful, indeed."

I gave him a despairing look, then went to help the

maid refold a blanket she'd dropped, forgetting Dimity's admonition never to intrude on a servant's work. My assistance seemed to embarrass the maid, who mumbled a word of thanks before scurrying off with her burden.

"Don't let Giddings see you helping the hired help," Oliver advised after she'd left. "He already suspects them of slacking off."

"Sorry," I said. "I'll try to remember that I'm a pampered guest." I started up the staircase, stopped, and turned to face Oliver again. "Claudia was terrific, wasn't she?"

"She always wanted to be a doctor," he said. "When she was little, she used me to practice bandaging. I spent many a fine summer afternoon bound up like a mummy."

"What changed her mind?" I asked.

"An active social life leaves little time for medical studies," Oliver answered, "and one needs an active social life to marry well. Now that she has married well, there's her husband's career to consider. What do you think he'd say if she declared her intention of launching her own career?"

" 'Good luck, honey'?" I ventured. "No, I guess not. Still, it seems like a waste. She was wonderful." I nodded to Oliver and continued up the stairs, my newfound respect for Claudia tinged with pity.

While the rest of us had panicked, she'd kept a cool head. She'd had the presence of mind to keep Nell warm and loosen her cravat. Her strident voice, so irritating in the drawing room, had pulled Nell from the dark well of oblivion. Claudia seemed to possess the sound instincts and quick reflexes needed to save lives. It saddened me to think that she'd used her gifts solely to secure a suitable mate. I wondered if it saddened her, too.

Oliver's soothing words and my sober reflections had momentarily distracted me from the shock of witnessing Nell's terrible fall, but I nearly came unglued again when I reached Annelise on the cell phone.

"You're *where?*" I said, sinking onto the edge of my bed.

"The stables at Anscombe Manor," she replied. "It's Saturday, Lori. The twins' riding lessons. Remember?"

"Riding lessons," I murmured, and ordered myself to calm down. The boys' "riding lessons" consisted of them making a few circuits around Anscombe Manor's hay-strewn paddock while seated on an ancient and extremely mild-mannered pony led at a sedate walking pace by Kit Smith on foot. It wasn't exactly the Kentucky Derby.

Annelise had grown accustomed to detecting agitation in my voice. "Is everything all right?" she asked.

"No, it's not," I said, and proceeded to tell her about Nell's riding accident.

"I'm so sorry to hear about Nell," she said when I'd finished. "But you don't have to worry about Will or Rob. They're wearing their helmets, and they've never fallen off old Bridey yet. Even if they did, Kit would catch them before they hit the ground."

Annelise wasn't telling me anything I didn't already know, but it was good to hear her say it aloud. It was even better to hear the twins bubble over with admiration for their peerless steed. Their joyful exuberance overcame any impulse I might have had to wrap them in cotton wool.

Our conversation was interrupted by a familiar click, and when Annelise got back to me, she said she'd better take the call.

"It's Bill," she told me. "I think he needs to hear from his children."

"I'm sure he does," I said, added a brief good-bye to the boys, and rang off.

I sat for a moment to collect my thoughts, then turned to Reginald. "You think Rob and Will would mind if I burned their riding boots?"

Reginald made no reply, but I knew what he would have said if he'd possessed the power of speech.

"They'd convince Kit to let them ride in sneakers," I acknowledged wryly, and thanked heaven that my sons had inherited a certain degree of stubbornness from me. They'd never let me smother them, no matter how hard I tried.

I returned the cell phone to my shoulder bag and went to the bathroom to wash my tear-blotched face. I was toweling off when I heard a loud thump on the bedroom door. When I opened the door, I found Simon standing in the corridor, holding a large silver tray laden with covered dishes.

"Sorry to kick the door," he said, "but as you can see, my hands are fully occupied."

"You shouldn't be carrying such a heavy load," I said.

He ignored my protest and swept past me into the room.

"I come bearing relatively good news," he announced. "Nell's injuries do not appear to be life-threatening."

"Thank God," I said, and heaved a quavering sigh of relief.

"I come bearing breakfast as well. Oliver told me you hadn't eaten." Simon placed the tray on the rosewood table and turned to face me. "He also told me you'd been weeping. I really can't have that, you know. Come here—but be gentle with me."

He opened his arms in a gesture that was more brotherly than seductive, so I went to him for a long, comforting hug.

"I know what you were feeling," he murmured. "The clutch at the heart . . . You'll think me mad, but I rang my son at Eton, just to hear his voice."

I tilted my head back to look up at him. "I did the same thing. You'll never guess where I found *my* sons."

When I told him, he responded with a sympathetic groan. "Poor old thing. I hope you're not planning to lock up their saddles."

"I briefly considered burning their boots," I confessed, "but what would be the point? A life without risk is no life at all."

Simon's midnight-blue eyes shifted slightly. They seemed to focus inward for a moment, as though my words had struck a chord, then he stepped away from me and said briskly, "Bill's a tremendous bully. I was deeply impressed. He simply shook the doctors by their stethoscopes until they coughed up a diagnosis. Nell has a dislocated shoulder, a broken collarbone, and mild concussion."

"Not great," I said, "but better than a fractured skull."

"Indeed," Simon agreed. "And now I must fly. I was dispatched to Hailesham to retrieve Bertie, who was left behind in the confusion."

"Go," I said, flapping my hands at him. "And thanks for the food. I think I might be able to find an appetite now."

When Simon had gone, I uttered a heartfelt prayer of thanksgiving, then sat at the writing table and made short work of the breakfast he'd so thoughtfully provided. I was too full of nervous energy to sit around twiddling my thumbs for the rest of the morning, so I grabbed my jacket and headed for the stables, in hopes of finding someone who'd confirm—or contradict—Nell's story about the flea-ridden horse blankets.

It seemed an insignificant detail, in light of what had happened, but after finding the strand of golden hair in the nursery, I needed to know, for my own peace of mind, if Nell had been telling the truth about burning the bundle of kerosene-soaked cloth.

An ominous shroud of gray clouds had covered the sun by the time I crossed the courtyard, and a chill wind snatched at the smoke rising from the workshops' chimneys. A half-dozen horses huddled for warmth in the rolling pasture beyond the greenhouses, but Deacon was not among them.

I found the dappled gray in a loose box in the imposing, neoclassical stone stable. Claudia was there, too, leaning on the box's half-door and gazing intently at Deacon.

"You found him," I said as I approached.

She glanced at me, then looked back at the horse. "He found his way here on his own. It's the strangest thing. He seemed . . . frightened."

"Of what?" I asked, standing beside her.

"Fences, apparently," she answered tersely. "He'll never make a hunter. Simon will have to get rid of him."

I studied the horse as he calmly nibbled the alfalfa pellets in the manger. "He went over the hurdles pretty willingly the first time Simon tried them."

"Deacon's headstrong and unreliable," Claudia declared. "If he were mine, I'd have him put down."

"Nell's going to be all right," I said hastily, and relayed Simon's report on Nell's injuries. I thought Claudia would be pleased by the news, but it only seemed to make her angrier.

"It was a stupid stunt," she said heatedly. "The shock could have killed Uncle Edwin. He's already had one heart attack. Another would finish him."

I gaped at her. "I'm sorry, Claudia, I had no idea that your uncle was ill. Does Derek know——"

"Derek has made it his business to know as little as possible about his father," Claudia broke in. "Uncle Edwin ceased long ago to look to him for either support or sympathy." She pushed herself away from the half-door and brushed her palms together lightly. "If you'll excuse me, Lori, I'm going to change. I'm absolutely filthy."

"Uh, Claudia, wait a minute." I thought fast, then improvised madly. "I wanted to ask—is there any part of the stables I should avoid? I heard a rumor that I might run into fleas."

"Not anymore," she informed me. "Nell burnt those dreadful old blankets yesterday. I wouldn't have touched them with a barge pole, but vermin don't faze Nell." As Claudia strode past me, she added haughtily, "I hope today's lesson will teach her to be a bit less fearless in future."

I stood outside of Deacon's loose box, lost in thought, until a gust of warm breath tickled the back of my neck. I turned and found myself face-to-face with the dappled gray. I cautiously raised a hand and stroked his velvet nose. He snuffled his appreciation.

"You don't seem headstrong to me," I murmured. "But I don't know much about horses."

I gave him a final pat, walked into the courtyard, and

paused. My gaze traveled from the neatly hedged pasture to the Victorian greenhouses, from the row of humble workshops to the intricate stonework gracing Hailesham's west facade.

Hundreds of country houses were demolished in the last century, Simon had told me. *Treasure houses the likes of which will never be seen again. It's a miracle that Hailesham survived, a miracle wrought by succeeding generations of my family. . . .*

I knew now, for certain, why the earl had called the cousins home.

The time had come to pass the torch to the next generation. He wasn't sure how much longer he had to live.

Sixteen

A sudden cloudburst sent me scrambling into the house. I was about to return to my room via the back staircase when I heard a faint trill of music coming from the drawing room. Someone was playing the grand piano.

Curious, I went to the entrance hall, slung my rain-spattered jacket over the staircase's wrought-iron balustrade, and opened the drawing room door. The red-haired maid sprang up from the piano bench, blushing crimson. I tried my best to appear nonthreatening, but I seemed destined to embarrass every temporary worker on Lord Elstyn's payroll.

"Sorry, madam, it won't happen again, madam, please don't tell Mr. Giddings," she sputtered.

"I won't breathe a word to Giddings," I said, "and there's no need to apologize. You play beautifully."

The maid fidgeted with her apron. "I'm only supposed to dust it, madam, but, well, it's such a fine instrument and it gets so little use. . . ."

"I understand," I told her. "Your secret's safe with me."

"Thank you, madam." She curtsied, grabbed her basket of cleaning supplies, and fled the room.

I went to the alcove, closed the keyboard lid, and was

halfway to the hall when I caught sight of someone sauntering up the graveled drive. I opened the French doors for a clearer view.

A tall young man clad in a waterproof parka, blue jeans, and muddy hiking boots strode jauntily up the drive, seemingly oblivious to the rain pelting his face and streaming from his backpack. I stared hard, then stared again. An astonished grin slowly spread across my face. I slammed the French doors shut, ran into the hall to grab my jacket, and pulled it on as I sprinted out the front door, down the stairs, and up the drive to meet him.

"Peter!" I shouted.

"Lori!" he shouted back, and lifted me from the ground in a bear hug when we collided.

"What are you doing here?" I demanded when he'd finally put me down. "Emma told me you were in New Zealand, chasing whales."

"I was." Peter shortened his strides so I wouldn't have to trot to keep up with him as we made our way to the house. "Emma got hold of me via a satellite linkup and said would I please come to Hailesham? Lost the signal before she could tell me why, but I came anyway. Hitched a flight to England with an RAF pal, got a lift from the base to the gates, and slogged in from there." He sucked in a great lungful of air. "Isn't it a *glorious* day?"

I laughed out loud. At twenty, Derek's son had shaken off all traces of the shy and fearful boy he'd once been. His sense of responsibility, however, remained intact. I doubted that many twenty-year-olds would drop everything and fly halfway around the world simply to oblige their stepmother.

"You must be the good news Emma's been hinting at," I told him.

"I certainly hope so. What happened to the turtle-dove?" he added, nodding toward the unsightly gap in the shrubbery.

"There was a fire," I answered noncommittally. "But there's something else you need to know right away."

I pulled Peter to a halt and told him about Nell's riding accident. He would have dumped his pack then and there and run to Salisbury, but I managed to convince him that his sister was in many good hands and that she would appreciate his visit more when her hospital room was less crowded.

He gazed at the hurdles and shook his head with grudging admiration. "My sister's never been afraid of a challenge," he said. "Mark my words: She won't be in hospital long. Come on." He took my arm. "Let's get in out of the rain."

Giddings was there to meet us when we splashed into the entrance hall.

"Giddings, you old trout," Peter cried, clapping the elderly manservant on the shoulder. "Why the long face? Hired help driving you mad, as usual?"

"One has no complaints about the temporary staff, Master Peter," Giddings said stiffly. "But one would have been grateful for advanced notice of your arrival."

"Room's not aired, eh?" Peter swung his dripping backpack to the floor, took off his parka, and knelt to remove his muddy boots. "Don't worry about it. I've been sleeping on a shelf for the past month."

"One must worry, sir," Giddings insisted. "One has one's standards."

"Sorry," Peter said, chastened. He stood. "I'll wait in the drawing room, shall I? Give you time to maintain your standards?"

Giddings snapped his fingers and two dark-suited men appeared. They relieved Peter of his pack, his boots, and his parka, took my jacket from me, and stood back.

"The fire has been lit in the drawing room, Master Peter," said Giddings, thawing slightly. "I've asked Cook to send up a hot meal. And may I say, on behalf of the entire staff, sir, what a great pleasure it is to have you among us again."

"Thank you, Giddings. And please thank Cook for me." Peter waggled his eyebrows mischievously. "Tell her I'll be down to pester her when she least expects it."

"I'll tell her, sir, but I doubt that it will come as a surprise." Giddings smiled at Peter with a warmth I hadn't known he possessed, but the smile vanished in an instant, and it was with great dignity that he opened the drawing room door, stood aside for Peter and me to enter, then closed the door behind us.

Peter strode over to the hearth, flopped onto the Aubusson carpet, and held his stockinged feet to the roaring fire. "Leaky boots," he explained. "My feet feel like dead fish. Don't suppose you have any idea why Emma asked me here."

I slipped my shoes off and sat beside him on the floor, my back against the settee, wondering what to say. "I can't be sure. . . ."

Peter had his father's deep blue eyes, but his hair was straight and as dark as Simon's. He brushed damp strands of it back from his forehead as he turned to me, a sober expression on his face.

"Give me your best guess," he said gently.

I wrapped my arms around my knees and told him what Claudia had told me about Lord Elstyn's heart attack. I told him that I thought the earl had called his family together to make some hard decisions about Hailesham's future. Finally, I told him that his father's relationship with his grandfather was as rocky as ever.

"I'm sure Derek doesn't know about the heart attack," I said. "If he did he wouldn't have . . ." I hesitated, then went on. "They had a shouting match yesterday. I'm sure Derek wouldn't have let it happen if he'd known about your grandfather's heart."

"I didn't know. Poor Grandfather . . . I've been away too long." Peter's voice was edged with self-reproach. The charge of neglect he'd leveled at himself seemed to weigh on him as heavily as the news of his grandfather's precarious health. He shook his head and loosed a regretful sigh before asking, "What were they shouting about?"

"Nell's crush on Kit," I said. "Your grandfather doesn't approve."

Peter lifted an eyebrow. "A wild understatement, I suspect. Grandfather has Prince William earmarked for Nell." He turned toward the fire, then gave me a speculative, sidelong glance. "It's rather more than a crush, you know."

"I know," I said.

Peter ruminated in silence, then said, "Emma wants me to shore up Dad's claim to the throne in case Grandfather has different ideas, is that it?"

I shrugged. "Maybe she just wants you to bang their heads together until they promise to stop behaving like a pair of stiff-necked idiots."

Peter's solemnity dissolved as he threw his head back and laughed. "My God, Lori, it's good to see you again."

Our conversation was interrupted by the arrival of Peter's hot meal. It was like watching a parade led by Grand Marshal Giddings, who silently directed a phalanx of servants to spread linen on the drum table, set it with covered dishes, rearrange the chairs, light candles, and generally turn the drawing room into a cozy dining room. When they'd finished, he dismissed them with a flick of his hand, bowed, and departed.

"There's enough here to feed a starving army," Peter said when we were seated at the table. "Dear old Cook, she still thinks I'm a growing boy."

I reached over and mussed his hair. "Something tells me you'll always be a growing boy."

We'd scarcely begun to uncover the dishes when Oliver and Claudia burst into the room. I watched in amazement as they threw their arms around Peter, pulled chairs up to the table, and fired questions at him about his travels.

Peter's presence seemed to transform them. Oliver's shyness was forgotten and Claudia's airhead act was put on the back burner. They ate with their fingers, teased each other, and swapped reminiscences about Peter's childhood peccadilloes that made him cringe even while his shoulders shook with laughter. The three cousins seemed determined to distract one another from the day's sobering events.

"I didn't *mean* to break the window in Grandfather's study," Peter protested. "I wasn't *aiming* at it when I threw the snowball."

"No, you were aiming at *me*," Oliver retorted.

"You see?" Peter said. "It wasn't my fault. If Oliver hadn't ducked—"

"You're *impossible,* Peter," Claudia interjected. "I hope you're not going to blame Oliver for the sheep in the library as well. . . ."

When we'd eaten our fill, we congregated on the carpet before the fire and the cousins continued their banter while I sat back and listened. Peter was clearly a great favorite, much missed by Claudia and Oliver when he was away and received with deep affection when he returned. They sat, entranced, while he spoke of recording whale songs, exploring the Amazon basin, and photographing Mount Etna's eruptions, and he responded with equal interest when they recounted recent events in their own, slightly less colorful lives.

As the gray and rainy afternoon dwindled into dusk, it struck me that Emma had been very wise to ask Peter to return to Hailesham. The earl might doubt Derek's devotion to the family, but he couldn't doubt Peter's. A blind man could see that Peter loved and was loved by his cousins. He combined Derek's sense of independence with Simon's charm and Oliver's humility. If it had been up to me, I would have chosen Peter to head the family.

Claudia was in the midst of describing her husband's most recent fund-raising dinner when Giddings appeared in the doorway.

"Yes, Giddings?" said Peter. "Are we making too much noise?"

"No, indeed, sir," the manservant replied. "I simply wished to draw your attention to Miss Eleanor's return." He swept a hand toward the French doors.

Peter was through the doors and onto the terrace before the rest of us had gotten to our feet. We followed him outside and watched wordlessly as a procession of vehicles rolled slowly up the graveled drive: Bill's Mercedes and the earl's limousine, with an ambulance bringing up the rear.

Peter pressed a hand to his mouth and swallowed hard but managed a crooked grin. "I told you, Lori. My sister may look like a butterfly, but she's built of solid oak."

"They wanted to keep Nell overnight for observation," Emma explained. "But she wanted to come home. And when an unstoppable force meets an immovable object . . ."

"Something's got to give," Bill finished. "The doctors were no match for Nell."

"Or for you, old man." Simon raised his glass to Bill.

Simon, Bill, Emma, Oliver, Claudia, Gina, and I sat in the drawing room, sipping single-malt whiskey and waiting for dinner to be served. No one except Gina had bothered to change into evening clothes, and though her floor-length aubergine gown was undeniably lovely, her insistence on formality seemed misplaced after such an emotionally draining day.

Two hours had passed since the ambulance attendants had carried Nell to her room on a stretcher and put her to bed. Derek hadn't left her side for a minute, and Peter had divided his time between his injured sister and his grandfather.

Lord Elstyn had gone straight upstairs to rest when he'd returned. Nothing was said of his heart condition, but the strain of seeing his golden girl laid low had evidently taken its toll.

The day at the hospital had frayed Gina's nerves as

well. Like Claudia, she was furious with Nell for endangering the earl's fragile health, and she made little effort to conceal her anger.

"I'm not entirely convinced that we should have given in to Nell," Gina observed. "One night in hospital seems a small price to pay for such reckless behavior."

"I'd hardly call Nell reckless," Bill observed mildly. "Anyone can fall off a horse."

"Nell's egregious lack of judgment resulted in an accident that caused my uncle great distress." Gina turned to Simon. "Did she ask your permission to take Deacon out?"

Simon frowned. "Nell doesn't need my permission to—"

"My point exactly," Gina interrupted. She eyed Bill coolly. "Nell has always been overindulged. If we continue to treat her like a spoilt child, she'll continue to behave like one. She must be taught that actions have consequences. You should not have interfered with the doctors' decision."

From the corner of my eye I saw Emma's lips tighten. If I'd been near her, I would have edged away, to keep clear of the crossfire.

"You must be mistaking my stepdaughter for someone else, Gina," she said with the deceptive calm of a stalking tigress. "I respect Nell's judgment because she's earned my respect. I know her to be an excellent horsewoman. Unfortunately, as Bill pointed out, accidents happen."

Gina opened her mouth to speak, but Emma cut her off ruthlessly.

"Although I'm grateful to Bill for speaking up on Nell's behalf," Emma continued, "I'm sure he'd be the first to remind you that Derek and I consulted with the doctors at length before consenting to Nell's release. We also consulted with Nell. You may mistrust your own child, Gina, but we have no reason to mistrust ours. When Nell told us she'd recover more quickly in familiar surroundings, we believed her." Emma's smile was etched in acid. "Any questions?"

Gina's response was preempted by Giddings, who chose the fraught moment to announce dinner. Gina pointedly ignored both Bill and Simon and took Oliver's arm before he'd quite gotten around to offering it. Bill rolled his eyes heavenward, then gallantly escorted Emma and Claudia into the dining room, leaving me to Simon's care.

"If Gina and Emma get into a food fight," I whispered to Simon, "I'm leaving."

"Not without me," he whispered back.

Seventeen

*D*inner was a tranquil affair, thanks to the mahogany table's extraordinary length. Oliver cleverly maneuvered Gina to one end while Bill deposited Emma at the other, thus reducing the risk of further hostilities. As an added precaution, all references to children and/or child-rearing practices were studiously edited from the general conversation.

Our collective peacemaking efforts paid off. The meal was completed without a single spoonful of soufflé becoming airborne. After dinner, Gina surprised me by asking Bill to join her in the earl's study. I'd expected her to boycott working with him after his nefarious behavior at the hospital, but her desire to please Lord Elstyn evidently outweighed her displeasure with Bill.

Claudia and Oliver departed soon after Bill and Gina, declaring their intention to keep the earl company until he fell asleep. When Emma elected to join Peter and Derek in their watch over Nell, Simon and I were left in sole possession of the drawing room.

It was a good night to be indoors, in front of a crackling fire. The rain had begun to fall with renewed vigor, and an occasional flash of lightning accompanied distant drumrolls of thunder.

After the others had gone, Simon poured tots of brandy into two glasses, handed one to me, and eased himself into an armchair facing the fire. I curled my legs beneath me and relaxed against the settee's cushioned arm, studying him while he drank. He'd poured himself a fairly hefty tot.

"You must be exhausted," I said.

"It has been rather a long day," he acknowledged. He rubbed his tired eyes with the heel of his hand. "On top of everything else, I was constantly afraid of running into the doctors who looked after me last night."

I nodded. "It would've been awkward if they'd asked about your bruised ribs in front of the others."

"Fortunately, a different shift had come on. No one recognized me." Simon sipped his drink and gazed into the fire. He seemed unusually subdued and introspective. "They recognized my uncle, though. It seems he had a heart attack four months ago. Gina knew about it, but I didn't. She told me at the time that he was in hospital for a routine examination and I, like a fool, believed her."

"Ah," I said, and focused my attention on my brandy. Simon's marriage seemed like a joke to me, but I doubted that the punch line would bring much joy to anyone.

Simon was silent for a moment. Then he said in a low voice, "It's my fault, Lori."

I looked up from my drink. "What's your fault?"

"When we were in the library yesterday, you asked if the note I showed you was the first I'd received," he said. "It was, in fact, the sixth. The others look exactly like the ones I've shown you. They began arriving at my home four months ago. I ignored the first two—"

"How could you ignore them?" I broke in.

Simon shrugged. "They seemed faintly ridiculous. They accused me of destroying Hailesham Park. How could I take such an accusation seriously, when nothing could be further from the truth?"

"What did you do with the other messages?" I asked.

"I brought them to Uncle Edwin." Simon slowly swirled the brandy in his glass. "He told me he'd take care of the problem. When the notes stopped coming, I thought he had."

"Until you found one waiting for you here," I said.

Simon tossed back the rest of his brandy. "I showed the notes to Uncle Edwin shortly before he went in for his supposedly routine examination. They must have disturbed him more than he let on. I believe they triggered his heart attack." He raised his arm and hurled his empty glass into the fire. "I wasn't satisfied with nearly killing my uncle," he muttered. "I had to try to kill my cousin as well."

I caught my breath and looked toward the shards of glass littering the hearth. "Simon," I said carefully, "you're not making any sense."

"I should have forbidden Nell to ride Deacon." His voice was taut with self-loathing. "I should have known the beast was dangerous after yesterday's debacle. I'm as much to blame for her injuries as I am for my uncle's failing health."

The pain in his voice went straight to my heart. I wanted to go to him and croon comforting words. Instead, I set my glass aside and said sternly, "Don't be stupid."

Simon turned his face away, as though I'd struck him, but I hammered on regardless.

"From what I've seen of your uncle's temper, I'd say he's been on the verge of a heart attack for a long time. If the poison-pen letters pushed him over the edge, then the blame lies with the lunatic who wrote them, not you. Look at me, Simon."

When he continued to avert his face, I got up from the settee and crossed to stand in front of him. He refused to meet my gaze.

"Nell's accident was . . . an accident," I insisted. "If you think you control life and death, you're giving yourself way too much credit. You may look like a god, Simon, but you're not God. You don't have that kind of power."

He closed his eyes. "It's easy for you to—"

"No, it's not easy," I shot back. "But I've been where you are. When my mother died, I was so racked with guilt that I didn't want to go on living, and if you think I'm going to let a friend start down the same path, then *you're* a lunatic. Stop wasting my time with this self-indulgent nonsense. We have work to do."

Simon looked up at me, suddenly alert. "You've found something?"

"You bet I have." I leaned over and took his hand. "Come with me to the nursery."

The paper and paste were still in the toy cupboard, and the vandalized books had not been removed from the bookcase. The poison pen hadn't yet attempted to cover his tracks.

When I told Simon about the curling strand of golden hair I'd discovered in *Romney to the Rescue,* he immediately shook his head and repeated, virtually word for word, each of Dimity's objections to viewing Nell as a possible suspect. He was so adamant in his defense of his cousin that I decided to keep Dimity's theories about Oliver to myself until after I'd revealed my most sensational find.

"I found it with the paste and paper," I explained, showing him the straight razor inlaid with the Elstyn family crest. "I'd say it was used to cut up the Malson books."

Simon's eyes narrowed. He took the razor from me and turned it over in his hands.

"It's one of Uncle Edwin's," he said, sliding his thumb over the tortoiseshell handle. "I remember watching him shave himself with it when I was very small, but he gave up cutthroats before I went away to school."

"What did he do with his old ones?" I asked.

Simon sank onto the window seat, his brow furrowed in concentration. "He gave them to his valet. He had one, years ago. . . . Chambers was his name. Uncle used to give him all sorts of castoffs—hats, suits, razors."

I breathed a sigh of relief as I put the defaced books back on the shelves. When it came to choosing a potential villain, I much preferred an unknown valet to a good-hearted brother.

I sat back on my heels. "Did Chambers dislike you?"

"No," said Simon. "He was fond of all of us, and we were fond of him. He took Oliver, Derek, and me fishing on his days off. We were keenly disappointed when he left."

My gaze drifted up to the seashells and birds' nests cluttering the bookcase's top shelves. "Why did Chambers leave?"

"As I recall, there was a general staff reduction the year after my aunt died," Simon answered, "a tightening of the fiscal belt. Chambers wasn't the only one to go."

"He was the only one who took your uncle's razor with him." I stood and wandered over to the rocking horse. A memory was flickering at the back of my mind, some-thing someone had said recently, but I couldn't quite zero in on it. "Did your uncle hire any new servants four months ago?"

"I've no idea. Giddings supervises staff hirings." Simon put a hand to his side and shifted his position on the win-dow seat, as if his bruised ribs were giving him trouble. "Why do you ask?"

"The first threats you received," I said, "the ones that began arriving four months ago—they looked exactly like the ones you've gotten here, right?"

"Yes." Simon's expression became thoughtful as his gaze fell on the bookcase. "The lettering was the same, which means that my persecutor has had access to those books for the past four months."

"Precisely. The razor ties Chambers to the books, and the books were used to make the nasty notes." I set the rocking horse rocking. "I think we should find out if your uncle's ex-valet has returned to Hailesham."

"Wouldn't he run the risk of being recognized?" Simon objected. "His was a very familiar face."

"Face . . ." I murmured, then clapped a hand to my forehead as the elusive memory snapped into focus. "That's it, Simon!"

"Sorry?" he said.

I scampered over to perch beside him on the window seat. "Old Mr. Harris, the master carpenter," I said excit-edly. "Emma and I were talking with him yesterday and he mentioned seeing a face he hadn't seen in *years*. It was one of the *old faces*. He said it took him *right back*. It must have been *Chambers*!"

Simon was unconvinced. "If old Mr. Harris recognized him, why wouldn't the rest of us?"

"The staff's trained to be invisible," I reasoned. "Apart from Giddings, they're nothing more than a bunch of guys in black suits who park cars and carry luggage. Can you tell one from another?"

"Probably not," Simon conceded.

I folded my arms in triumph. "Chambers couldn't ask for a better disguise."

"Why would Chambers accuse me of destroying Hailesham?" Simon asked, bewildered.

"Let's find out if he's here first," I suggested. "We'll worry about motivation later."

Simon promised to speak with Giddings in the morning, slipped the razor into his own pocket, and looked toward the vandalized Malson books. He smiled.

"You seem as intent on avenging Romney Rat," he said, "as you are on protecting me."

"I don't like seeing either one of you hurt." I sighed and shook my head. "When I found those books, I was furious. Cutting them to bits is like burning the turtledove—a barbaric act."

"A crime against civilization?" Simon teased.

"Yes," I replied firmly.

"I'm beginning to think you love Hailesham as much as I do," he said.

"I love the idea of Hailesham," I allowed.

"What do you mean?" he asked.

I rubbed the tip of my nose, folded my legs beneath me, and tried to explain. "The world is such a mess. . . . Why not preserve the bits of it that aren't a mess?"

"Sounds fairly elitist to me," Simon commented.

"Maybe it is, but so what?" I looked at the wonderful rocking horse. "The poorest people on earth carve wood, mold clay, sculpt stone—because the human spirit craves beauty. It thirsts for splendor. Its dreams reach beyond the ordinary. I'll never go to the moon, but I'm glad someone went there. Even if I'd never seen Hailesham, I'd want to know that such a place exists. The mere idea of it feeds my dreams."

Simon gazed at me in silence, then put his hand on mine. "Lori, my dear, you are a hopeless romantic."

I grinned sheepishly. "I prefer to think of myself as a hopeful one."

Simon patted my hand, then folded his in his lap. He cocked an ear toward the rain lashing the windowpanes behind us and said, "Sorry about the self-indulgent nonsense."

"There's nothing to be sorry about," I told him. "You're tired, you're aching, and you've spent the day watching two people you love suffer." I got up, turned off the wall lamp, and proceeded Simon into the dimly lit corridor. "You need to drink a glass of warm milk and go to bed."

He gripped my arm and swung me around to face him. His midnight-blue eyes gleamed softly in the semi-darkness as he murmured, "I don't suppose you'd care to join me."

For a fleeting moment I wanted nothing more than to rise up on tiptoe and respond with sweet abandon to his invitation, but the moment passed and my feet remained firmly on the ground.

"In your condition?" I tossed my head. "I'd lose my status as your honorary nanny."

"I *refuse* to think of you as my nanny," he stated flatly.

I smiled up at him. "Then think of me as your friend."

"Friend." He tilted his head to one side and pronounced the word experimentally. "Friend is better than nanny, I suppose."

"Much better." I took his hand and hooked it in the crook of my arm as we strolled toward the staircase. "But if you ever ask me to go to bed with you again, Simon, I reserve the right to box your ears."

I left Simon at his bedroom door, then sailed straight through my firelit room and into Bill's, but my husband was still burning the midnight oil with Gina. I gazed at his pillow reflectively and decided, on behalf of all hopeful romantics everywhere, to leave a note on his bed that might lure him into mine when he finally finished his working day.

Enticing phrases filled my mind as I returned to the writing table in my room in search of notepaper. I was giggling over a particularly sultry phrase when the drapes billowed inward.

I stepped toward them, wondering who'd left the window open, then recoiled in terror as a shadowy figure lunged at me, raising a clenched fist.

Eighteen

My assailant sneezed.

The shriek that had risen halfway up my throat emerged as a garbled "God bless you!"

"Thanks," said the shadowy figure. He raised his fist again to cover a second sneeze. "Do you have a tissue? My handkerchief's drenched."

A log fell on the fire, sparks flew, and I caught a glimpse of my attacker's face. I knew those delicately carved features. The fine, straight nose, the curving lips, and the wide-set violet eyes belonged to the most beautiful man I'd ever met.

"*Kit?*" I squeaked.

"Keep your voice down," Kit urged. He stepped closer and asked, "How's Nell?"

"She's banged up," I said. "But they let her come home this evening, so——"

"She's *here*? Is she *alone*?" he demanded sharply.

"No," I replied, dizzied by the rapid-fire interrogation. "Derek, Emma, and Peter are with her."

He seemed to relax. "About that tissue . . ."

I leaned on the desk for a moment, to recover from Kit's heart-stopping entrance, then took a packet of tissues from my shoulder bag and thrust it at him.

"I should give you a kick in the backside for scaring me like that," I said in a heated whisper.

"Sorry." He blew his nose and tossed the crumpled tissue in the wastebasket. "I thought you might be another maid. Thousands have been tramping through here—turning down the bed, lighting the fire, freshening the vases. I had to slip out onto the balcony when the red-haired one hoovered the carpet."

I peered at him more closely. A waterproof parka had protected his dark blue crew-neck sweater from the storm, but his work boots and blue jeans were sopping wet, and rivulets of rain drizzled from his short-cropped gray hair.

"You're soaked," I said in dismay.

"I am a bit damp," he admitted. "I had to park the van a couple of miles away and hike in."

I motioned toward the hearth. "Go and sit by the fire while I find something of Bill's for you to change into."

He knew better than to argue and we both knew why. Kit Smith hadn't always been gainfully employed as the Harrises' stable master. When I'd first met him, he'd been homeless, starving, and half dead from a combination of hypothermia and pneumonia. His encounter with the grim reaper had been close enough to turn his hair gray at the ripe young age of thirty. I'd been a little overprotective of him ever since.

It took five minutes for Kit to change into dry socks and a pair of Bill's twill trousers. He and Bill were much the same height—just over six feet—but Kit was the leaner of the two, so I added one of Bill's leather belts to the ensemble. While Kit toweled his hair dry, I hung his wet clothes from the mantelpiece, dragged a pair of armchairs close to the fire, pulled a blanket from the bed, and wrapped it around him. We spoke in lowered voices as we sat facing each other across the hearth.

"I'd phone the kitchen for a pot of hot chocolate," I said, "but it's past Cook's bedtime."

"I've stopped sneezing," he said meekly.

I ducked my head and smiled, but my amusement was short-lived. I couldn't believe that Kit had been so foolhardy as to come to Hailesham Park.

"How did you get into my room?" I asked.

"You gave Annelise a fairly detailed description of the view from your balcony," he explained. "I climbed up the stonework, spotted Reginald, and knew I'd found the right place."

"You climbed the stonework," I repeated. "After walking two miles. Through the storm."

"I had no choice." Kit held his hands out to the fire. "Lord Elstyn thinks I've trifled with his granddaughter's affections. Can you imagine what would've happened if I'd knocked on his front door?"

"He did mention something about *shooting you* if you set foot on his property," I said with some asperity.

"I know I'm not welcome here, Lori, but I had to come." Kit's expression was grave as his eyes met mine. "Nell's in danger."

The hairs on the back of my neck prickled, but I waited for him to go on. He hunched forward in his chair, his elbows resting on his knees, his hands clasped tightly together.

"When Annelise told me about your call this morning, I knew something was wrong. The horse hasn't been born that can throw Nell, under normal circumstances."

Though Emma had said much the same thing in response to Gina's gibes, Kit's opinion carried more weight. Emma might be blinded by her stepmaternal love for Nell, but Kit the stable master would neither under- nor overrate his pupil's abilities. When it came to horsemanship, Kit was utterly clear-sighted.

"I thought of ringing you and asking you to look into it," he went on, "but you've never been comfortable around horses."

"I wouldn't know what to look for," I agreed.

"That's why I had to come. I had to find out what had really happened." Kit drew the blanket more closely around him. "I went to the stables first, to gauge Deacon's temperament. The horse is sound, Lori. Spirited, yes, but nothing Nell can't handle."

"Deacon's thrown two good riders in two days," I pointed out.

"It's not his fault," said Kit.

I didn't understand what he was getting at. "If it's not Nell's fault, or Deacon's, then—"

"The hurdles." Kit shrugged the blanket from his shoulders, stood, and rummaged in the cargo pocket of his dripping parka. When he turned back to me, he was holding a tangled web of fine electrical wiring.

"Flashbulbs," he said, handing the wire to me. "Remote-controlled flashbulbs. I found the wire wound among the ivy on the hurdles. Someone must have hidden the bulbs there and set them off when Deacon approached. The flashes terrified him and he panicked. No one could have stayed on him after that."

I stared at the tiny bulbs, horrified. "Claudia said he seemed frightened," I muttered. "And Simon . . . Simon told me he saw stars when he fell. He must have caught a glimpse of . . . *these*."

Kit resumed his seat. "It was an intentional act of sabotage, Lori. Someone was trying to hurt Nell."

I closed my eyes and watched the accident unfold once more in memory. I saw Deacon's steady strides, the fluttering ivy, the long-legged rider, the helmet, the black coat, the tall boots. . . .

"No," I said, shuddering. "It's not Nell they're trying to hurt. It's *Simon*."

I dropped the wire on the floor, reached into my pocket, and withdrew the poison-pen notes. With trembling hands, I unfolded the note Simon had discovered after his fall.

"'A pity you didn't land on your head. Better luck next time.'" I was filled with a sickening sense of failure as I read the words aloud. "Simon thought it was a harmless bit of mockery, but I should have known it was more serious. I should have seen it coming."

"What should you have seen?" Kit asked. "What's going on?"

I looked from the note to the bulb-festooned wire, then sat forward in my chair and carefully outlined to Kit my theory about Lord Elstyn's plan to disinherit Derek in favor of Simon.

"I think some lunatic's trying to protect Derek by getting rid of Simon," I continued. "Simon's received a series of nasty messages similar to these." I handed both notes to Kit and told him about the torched turtledove. "When Simon ignored the notes, someone set fire to the topiary. When he refused to be intimidated by the fire——"

"The lunatic rigged the flashbulbs," Kit said grimly.

I nodded. "When Deacon panicked yesterday, Simon was so badly hurt that he wasn't able to ride today."

"That must be why Nell took Deacon out this morning," Kit commented. "She wanted to prove to everyone that he's manageable."

"From a distance, when they're on horseback, it's hard to tell one cousin from another," I explained. "The maniac must have mistaken Nell for Simon and tried the flashbulb trick again: 'Better luck next time,'" I repeated bitterly.

Kit returned the notes to me and I put them back in my pocket.

"Why hasn't Simon gone to the police?" he asked.

"He didn't want to open the door to a public scandal," I replied. "He wanted to expose his persecutor privately. And we may be on the right track. . . ."

I recounted my discovery of the vandalized books and the razor and concluded with my suspicions regarding Chambers, the earl's ex-valet. Kit listened without interruption, but when I'd finished, he shook his head.

"I understand Simon's reluctance to involve the police," he said, "but it's gone too far. He could have been killed yesterday. Nell could have been killed today. Simon must notify the authorities and ask for a proper investigation. If he won't . . ."

"I will," I promised.

Kit knelt to stir the fire. After he returned the poker to the stand, he remained kneeling, with his back to me. We gazed into the rising flames, absorbed in our own private meditations. Kit was the first to break the silence.

"Will you take me to her?" he asked.

The request snapped me out of my reverie. "To Nell?"

He nodded, but his gaze remained fixed on the fire. "I

need to see her, Lori. I may not be in love with her, but she's . . . dear to me. I've been so worried. I have to see her before I go."

"Derek and the others will be with her," I reminded him.

"All the better," he said. "Please take me to her."

"I don't know where her room is," I said.

"I do." Kit sat on the floor and pulled his knees to his chest. A half-smile played on his lips, as though he was recalling a fond memory. "When I first arrived at Anscombe Manor, I was too weak to do much of anything. Nell and Bertie used to keep me company. She brought me books and kittens and plum cake, and she told me all about her illustrious grandfather and the glories of Hailesham Park." The firelight shone in Kit's violet eyes as he turned his face up to me. "Her room overlooks the terraced gardens. It's in the south wing, across from the painting of the lady in pink slippers."

I took a deep breath. "Okay," I said, "but let me go first. Lord Elstyn'll aim more carefully if I'm standing in front of you. I hope."

Nineteen

F scrawled a brief note to Bill, telling him that I'd be back shortly—with explanations—and propped it against the black onyx urn that was holding Kit's parka in place on the mantelpiece. Kit waited while I searched the corridor for signs of life, then followed me as I led the way to the south wing. We were crossing the landing when the sound of voices floated up to us from the stairwell.

"It may be legal, Gina, but you know as well as I do that it's wrong," Bill was saying.

"Right and wrong are abstract concepts," Gina observed. "I'm concerned solely with legality."

"I'll continue to fight you on this," Bill warned.

Gina's throaty laughter was filled with disdain. "Your devotion to a lost cause is truly touching."

"It's not lost yet," said Bill. "When we meet tomorrow, I'm going to insist on . . ."

I'd have given ten sacks of silver to continue eavesdropping on their conversation, but their voices were growing louder, which meant that they were heading straight toward us. I didn't need a crystal ball to tell me what would happen if Gina saw me leading an oddly dressed stranger in the general direction of Nell's bedroom, so Kit and I hotfooted it into the south wing at top speed.

"Pink slippers, pink slippers, pink slippers," I muttered as we dashed past the paintings lining the long corridor. We were halfway to the end when I spotted an improbably well-dressed shepherdess with a simpering smile, a beribboned crook, and . . .

"Pink slippers!" I whispered excitedly, pointing at the telltale footgear, but Kit had already disappeared through the door opposite the shepherdess. I glanced toward the staircase, distinctly heard Bill clear his throat, and scrambled after Kit, closing the door behind us. I leaned against it to catch my breath while my gaze moved slowly around the room.

I saw nothing to indicate the presence of a teenager—no gaudy posters, no electronics, no mess. The decor reflected the refined taste of a mature woman who knew her own mind and trusted her own judgment. It was exactly what I would have expected of Nell.

The walls were hung with exquisite hand-painted paper: gnarled boughs clouded with apple blossoms in the most delicate shades of ivory, rose, and celadon. The furniture came from many periods, as if each piece had been chosen by virtue of its graceful lines or handsome fabrics instead of its dull conformity to one particular style.

The creamy marble mantelpiece echoed that in the drawing room with its miniature pillars and porticoes, and the half-canopied bed was draped in a sumptuous, pale green damask edged with gold braid. Nell's chocolate-brown teddy bear and Derek's battered gray elephant leaned companionably against each other on a fringed

cushion at the foot of the bed, but they were there as cher-
ished friends, not toys.

A silver-framed black-and-white photograph of Emma,
Derek, and Peter sat on the bedside table, beneath a
parchment-shaded lamp that shed a soft pool of light
over a grouping of three chairs that now stood empty.
The dim lamp sent furtive gleams through Nell's tumble
of golden curls.

She lay with her eyes closed, half raised on a mound of
pillows, her right arm resting atop the embroidered coverlet, the left tucked out of sight beneath it. Spills of lace
fell from her white nightgown's collar and cuffs. The
gown's high neckline hid the bandages that wrapped her
broken collarbone and dislocated shoulder.

She looked as pale as a dove, as frail as frost, as vulner-
able as a sleeping kitten. The rose-petal blush had left her
lips, and there were shadows beneath her eyes that had
never been there before. I heard Kit exhale raggedly, as if
it hurt him to see her suffering. He turned and was about
to quit the room when Nell spoke.

"Kit," she said, in a voice so weak that it was nearly
swallowed by the pouring rain.

Kit heard her. He stood motionless for a moment, then
slowly turned and walked to Nell's side. I know it was
wrong of me, but as he stood over her I couldn't help
imagining how beautiful their children would be, if
only . . .

"Hullo, Nell," he said.

She opened her eyes and gazed up at him. "I knew
you'd come. That's why I sent the others away."

"You shouldn't be alone," Kit scolded gently.

"I'm not." Nell managed a ghost of a smile, but in the next moment her dark blue eyes were glazed with tears. "Claudia wants to shoot Deacon."

"I won't let her," said Kit. "It wasn't Deacon's fault."

Nell's chest heaved. "Mine?" she asked in a very small voice.

"No." Kit reached down to brush away a tear that had trickled down Nell's silken cheek. "There were wires, lights—someone tampered with the hurdles. When you're stronger, Lori will explain, but you must rest now."

"Simon's demon," Nell whispered. Her breath quickened. "You must tell Grandpapa. He knows—"

"Hush." Kit placed his hand on the pale one that lay atop the coverlet. "Lori will speak with your grandfather. Your only task is to get well. You need to be strong enough to drive Rosie's sleigh when you come home at Christmas."

"I'm not coming home," said Nell.

"No?" Kit gave her a troubled, searching look as his hand drifted to his side, but when he spoke again his voice was calm and soothing. "The Seine is lovely in winter. You must try to be well enough by then to savor its beauty. Sleep now and dream of Paris."

Nell's steady gaze never left his face. "I'll dream," she murmured, "but not of Paris."

Kit stepped back. "I . . . I should go," he faltered. "Good-bye, Nell."

Nell closed her eyes and whispered, *"Au revoir,* Kit."

Kit swallowed hard, then stumbled toward the door. He would have blundered past me and into the corridor if I hadn't held him back while I made sure no one was out there. He maintained a preoccupied silence until we found

Bill waiting for us in my room, when he said, without pre-amble:

"Nell's not coming home for Christmas."

Bill's eyes shifted to mine. When I responded with a minute shrug, he said, "I imagine her studies are—"

"It's nothing to do with her studies." Kit looked stricken. He sank onto an armchair by the fire and leaned his forehead on his hands. "It's me. She left Anscombe Manor because of me, and she's staying away because of me. I'm keeping her apart from her family, her home. It can't go on."

"It won't." Bill gestured for me to keep back as he crossed to sit in the chair facing Kit's. He must have been yearning for sleep after the long and trying day, but there was no trace of impatience in his voice, only kindness and understanding. "Nell loves you Kit, and she knows you don't love her. It's taken a tremendous amount of courage for her to accept the truth and move on."

Kit raised his head to look at Bill. "I don't think she's moving on."

"She will," said Bill, "given time and distance and a university full of handsome young Frenchmen. You'll see. She'll come home at Easter with Pierre or Jean-Luc or François in tow, and you'll have to reconcile yourself to being just another uncle figure in her life."

Kit sighed. "If I could believe that . . ."

"Believe it." Bill gave Kit an encouraging smile, then asked, "Are you planning to spend the night here? Because if you are—"

"I'm not," said Kit. "I brought the van."

"He parked it two miles away," I put in.

Bill rose. "I'll drive you to the van."

"It's nearly one in the morning," Kit protested.

"I'm too restless to sleep," said Bill. "Maybe the drive will calm me down."

Kit reluctantly accepted the offer and went into the dressing room to change out of Bill's trousers and into his own. When he was safely out of earshot, I put my arms around my husband's neck.

"You are my idea of the perfect man," I said, running my fingers through his hair. "But Kit's right about Nell."

"Then let's hope I'm right, too." He pulled me close, then went to fetch his raincoat.

Kit returned, clad once again in his jeans, parka, and boots. He retrieved the bulb-festooned wire from the floor and handed it to me.

"You'll speak with Lord Elstyn," he said.

"I'll speak with everyone." I gave him a tight hug. "Thank you, Kit. I dread to think what might have happened if you hadn't come here tonight."

"It's in your hands now." Kit turned as Bill hastened back from the dressing room. "Ready?"

"Let's go," said Bill, and led the way into the corridor.

When the two men had gone, I wound the wire into a coil, placed it next to Reginald on the bedside table, and picked up the blue journal.

Twenty

*C*hambers?

    I carried the blue journal to the armchair nearest the hearth, where I could watch Aunt Dimity's fluid script unfurl by firelight.

I don't recall ever hearing the name, but there's no reason I should. Edwin would hardly discuss his valet with me. I'm somewhat puzzled by Simon's instant recollection of the man. Valets don't, as a rule, interact with children.

"Chambers did," I told her, settling into the chair. "He used to spend his days off with Simon, Oliver, and Derek. He took them fishing."

Fishing? With three little boys? How peculiar. I've never encountered a valet who would sacrifice his day off to the dubious joys of baiting hooks for three rambunctious little boys.

"Maybe he was trying to impress his employer," I suggested.

A valet impresses his employer by attending to his employer's needs, not those of the children in the house. Take it from one who knows, my dear: Chambers's behavior would have been considered rather eccentric.

"He may have been eccentric then," I commented, "but he's bonkers now."

As I've said from the start, poison pens are notoriously unstable. Chambers—if Chambers is the culprit—has merely proved my point. When indirect action failed, he escalated his campaign. What had been annoying very nearly became murderous. Thank heavens for Kit. If it weren't for him, we might never have discovered the wicked act of sabotage that injured both Simon and Nell.

"It wasn't easy for Kit," I murmured pensively. "Seeing Nell, I mean."

He was troubled to discover that her time abroad has not lessened her affection for him.

My eyebrows rose. "How did you know?"

I know Nell. She's not one to give her heart lightly, and you've told me that Kit believes himself incapable of reciprocating her affection. It's a most unfortunate situation. I feel for them both.

"Me, too." I suddenly remembered a tidbit that had slipped my mind in my preoccupation with Kit. "When Kit told Nell about the hurdles, Dimity, she muttered something about Simon's demon. She became agitated and told him to speak with Lord Elstyn—"

Royal-blue ink spattered the page as Dimity's words raced across it. *He didn't agree to do so, did he?*

"Of course not," I said. "He told her I'd speak with the earl. But what did she mean by 'Simon's demon'? Do you think she knows about the poison pen?"

It would amaze me if she did not. Nell is highly intelligent as well as observant, and she's intimately familiar with everyone involved. Such emotionally charged events could scarcely take place beneath her nose without her catching the scent. The handwriting paused briefly, then resumed. *You remember the strand of golden hair you found in the vandalized books?*

"How could I forget it?" I said, recalling the foolish suspicions I'd harbored about Nell.

Perhaps Nell discovered the damage done to those books before you did. She might have taken it into her head to piece together the missing letters and deduce the messages that might be created with them. Or, if you prefer a simpler solution, Edwin may have taken his granddaughter into his confidence. You did mention that Edwin was aware of his nephew's persecution.

I nodded slowly. "Simon gave three of the nasty notes to him."

I wonder if Simon offended Chambers in some way—if he inadvertently caused Chambers to lose his position as Edwin's valet?

"I don't think so," I said. "Chambers wasn't the only servant to lose his job. Simon told me that the earl fired most of the staff the year after his wife died because of financial troubles."

Simon's mistaken. The troubles weren't financial, Lori. They were emotional.

"What do you mean?" I asked.

The first time I met Edwin was when I came to Hailesham to thank him for an extremely generous donation he'd made to a Westwood Trust hospice for terminal cancer patients. He'd made the donation in his wife's name.

I sat forward in my chair. "Did Derek's mother die of cancer?"

Sadly, yes. Edwin did everything in his power to save her. Lady Hailesham spent a year in London, undergoing every sort of treatment, but it was to no avail.

"I had no idea," I said. "Derek didn't mention a thing to me about cancer."

I'm not surprised. Lady Hailesham's illness was a terrible blow to the family. Edwin may not have married for love, but love grew nonetheless. Edwin adored his wife. After her death, he could never bring himself to look at another woman, let alone remarry. His social life came to a standstill for a number of years, while he buried himself in building his empire. Without his wife at his side, he couldn't bear to host parties or welcome guests to Hailesham Park. That's why he reduced the staff.

I scanned Dimity's words with a growing sense of incredulity. "Derek told me that his mother went to live in London because she hated his father."

I beg your pardon?

"Derek believes that his mother left Hailesham to get away from his father," I said. "He's always believed it, ever since he was a little boy. That's why he hates his father. That's why he changed his name and rejected his family and . . . and *everything*." I gripped the journal tightly. "Are you telling me that Derek altered the direction of his entire life simply because no one told him the truth about his mother's death?"

A breeze ruffled the flames in the fireplace, as if Dimity had breathed a mournful sigh.

Derek was so young when Lady Hailesham became ill— scarcely six years old. Edwin didn't want him to remember his mother as she was after the radiation, the chemotherapy, the surgery, and the disease itself had taken their toll. Afterward, he found it difficult to speak of her to anyone.

"He spoke to you," I commented.

I believe I was the first person in whom he confided. I'd worked in the hospice, you see. Few deaths are kind, but cancer can be very cruel, indeed. I'd sat with many families while they watched someone they loved diminished, then destroyed by the disease. I had some understanding of Edwin's pain, but I urged him nonetheless to tell his son the truth. He said he would, when Derek was a bit older.

"He must have waited too long," I said. "By the time he got around to talking to his son, his son was no longer willing to listen." I looked toward the rain-dashed windows. "What a mess."

When you speak with Edwin about the poison pen, you must also tell him about Derek.

"Me?" I gulped as I read Dimity's injunction. "I'm not sure the earl will appreciate an outsider like me reopening old wounds."

The wound is infected, Lori. It must be reopened if it is to heal. You will speak with him?

"I'll try." I glanced at the door. "But I'll speak with Bill first. He should be back any minute now."

I'll leave you to it, then. I must say that your stay at Hailesham Park is proving to be as complicated as your sojourn in Northumberland. I don't think you're cut out for peaceful holidays, my dear.

I smiled wryly as the curving lines of royal-blue ink faded from the page. When I called to mind the strange and sometimes frightening things that had happened to me the last time I'd left home, I was forced to agree with Dimity: I wasn't a fun-in-the-sun type of gal.

I returned the blue journal to the bedside table, reached for Reginald, and stretched out on the bed. I listened to the rain as it whooshed in sheets against the windowpanes and tried to think of a painless way to rip open an old, infected wound.

The next thing I knew, Bill was kissing me awake. I wasn't sure how long he'd been back, but he'd already changed into his pajamas.

"Time to put on your jammies," he said.

"Don't need jammies." I set Reginald aside, gave Bill my steamiest smile, and began unbuttoning my silk blouse.

When we eventually got around to talking, I told Bill exactly why my stay at Hailesham Park had been anything but boring. I expected him to be upset with me for not confiding in him sooner, but he wasn't. He respected me for keeping my promise to Simon, and he understood Simon's fear of scandal. He also acknowledged that he hadn't given me many opportunities to speak privately with him since we'd arrived at Hailesham.

"I'll pave the way for you to meet with Lord Elstyn," he promised. "But no matter what he says, Simon will have to notify the police."

"You don't have to convince me." I snuggled closer to him. "There's something else I need to tell you, Bill."

My husband emitted an aggrieved groan. "It's not about you and Simon, is it? I realize that he's a charmer, Lori, but—"

"It's not about Simon," I interrupted with mild indignation—very mild indignation, since both Bill and I were acutely aware of my less-than-stellar track record with charmers. "It's about you and Gina. For a while there I was under the impression that maybe the two of you might've . . . well, you know . . . had something going."

Bill sat bolt upright in bed. "Me and *Gina*? Are you *insane*?"

"You muttered her name one night in your sleep," I attempted to explain, "so I thought—"

"If I muttered her name," Bill declared, "it was because I was dreaming of *strangling* her. How could you possibly think that I would *ever* . . ." He sputtered into incoherence.

"She's beautiful," I ventured. "She's smart. She's a lawyer. You have a lot in common."

Bill rolled his eyes and raised his palms to the heavens, then swung around and pinned me to the bed. "I'm not saying I could never be attracted to another woman, love, but never, not in ten thousand years, could I ever be attracted to a woman like Gina." His voice softened. "Why would I settle for smarts and beauty when I've got all of that and so much more with you?"

It was my turn for incoherence, but Bill had no trouble whatsoever understanding my reply.

Twenty-one

*B*ill and I were awakened the next morning by a tap at the bedroom door. While Bill searched for his pajamas, I pulled the covers up to my chin and gazed blearily toward the balcony. The wispy gray light filtering through the glass told me that dawn had barely broken.

Bill finally managed to locate his pajama bottoms in a tangled heap under the bed, pulled them on, and went to answer the door. The red-haired maid stood in the corridor beside a wheeled serving cart.

"I beg your pardon, sir," she said, courteously averting her gaze from my husband's rather fetching torso, "but to expedite the morning's business, Lord Elstyn has ordered breakfast to be served upstairs today. He requires your presence, sir, and that of Mrs. Willis, in the study in one hour."

"My wife's name is Ms. Shepherd," Bill told her, "but I take your meaning. We'll be there."

The maid motioned toward the cart. "Shall I . . . ?"

"I'll take it." Bill pulled the cart into the room, thanked the maid, and closed the door. He folded his arms across his bare chest and studied the covered dishes in silence.

"I'm all for room service," I grumbled, reaching for my robe, "but couldn't it come at a more reasonable hour?"

"I detect Gina's hand in this," said Bill, nodding at the cart. "It would serve her purpose to have everyone off balance today."

"It's Elstyn business." I yawned hugely. "What does she want with me?"

"I don't know." Bill pushed the cart between the two armchairs near the hearth and beckoned for me to join him. "But I intend to be well fed and wide-awake when I find out."

As we descended the main staircase, Bill's expression became as severe as his black three-piece suit, as if he were girding himself to do battle. While he'd dressed for business, I'd dressed for warmth, pairing a cream-colored cashmere sweater with a tailored tweed blazer and skirt. I carried my shoulder bag as well. It held the saboteur's wire, which I planned to show the earl when the morning's meeting was over.

The study lay beyond the billiards room, in a part of the house I hadn't yet explored. Its floor-to-ceiling windows overlooked the north end of the courtyard, where the workshops stood and where a young and rascally Peter had once hurled a snowball at Oliver—and missed.

The study was a room of modest proportions and masculine decor. It reminded me of an old-fashioned gentlemen's club, with its oak-paneled walls, shiny oxblood leather chairs, hunting prints, longcase clock, and gold velvet drapes. A fire danced in the oak-manteled hearth at the far end of the room, and the faint scent of cigar smoke seemed to linger in the air.

The chairs had been arranged in a half circle facing a massive mahogany desk that stood before the windows. When Bill and I arrived, all but four of the chairs were occupied. Peter sat at the center of the half circle, with Derek and Emma to his right and Claudia and Oliver to his left. Gina, however, stood behind the desk, examining a file folder, and Simon stood before the hearth, with his back to her.

Only Nell and Lord Elstyn were missing. I suspected the earl of orchestrating a dramatic entrance for himself but seriously doubted that Nell would leave her bed to attend the meeting.

Every face turned toward us when we entered the room, including that of the red-haired maid, who was moving from person to person, offering cups of tea. She didn't have many takers. Simon accepted a cup, for politeness' sake, evidently, because he immediately placed it on the mantelshelf, untasted. When the others declined refreshment, the maid curtsied and left the room.

Gina favored Bill with a brief, dismissive glance as he took a seat beside Derek, then returned her attention to the file folder. I paused at Emma's side to ask after Nell.

"Nell is Nell," Emma replied with a wry smile. "She wouldn't let us sit with her through the night because *her* accident had taken so much out of *us*."

"We looked in on her, of course," Derek added, "and every time we did she was asleep, so we're fairly confident that we made the right decision when we allowed her to leave the hospital."

"There's no question about it." I reassured them both, then crossed to stand with Simon before the hearth.

"Tea?" he offered, nodding at the cup on the mantelshelf. "I've no stomach for it this morning."

"No, thanks," I said, and edged closer to him. "Have you spoken with Giddings about Chambers?"

"Haven't had the chance," he answered, sotto voce. "No one seems to know where Giddings is." He peered at me curiously. "I'm rather surprised to see you here. Pleased, but surprised."

"Not half as surprised as—" I fell silent as the study door flew open.

Lord Elstyn strode into the room. He seemed to have recovered his energy. Looking neither left nor right, he went directly to his desk and seated himself behind it. Gina, file folder in hand, promptly sat in the armchair next to Oliver's—mirroring Bill's position at Derek's side—but Simon and I remained standing, though we turned to face the earl. No one made a sound.

Lord Elstyn rested his folded hands on the desk and tapped the tips of his thumbs together. He appeared to be pondering his opening remarks, which, to judge by his stern expression, would deal with weighty matters— such as the disinheritance of his only child.

"I apologize for rousing you at such an inhospitable hour," he began, "but a situation has arisen that may affect all of us."

Gina's eyes narrowed slightly, as if the earl had inexplicably departed from an agreed-upon script. Bill, too, looked faintly puzzled, but the others simply waited for the earl to go on.

"In speaking with my granddaughter this morning," he continued, "I learned certain facts of a most alarming nature."

Lord Elstyn's penetrating gaze fell on my shoulder bag, then shifted to my face. I quaked when he held his hand out to me, and heard vague mutterings from the others as I approached the desk, opened my bag, and handed the coiled wire to him. Though flustered, I kept my mouth shut. I didn't know what Nell had told him about the wire's discovery, but I wasn't going to give Kit away.

The earl, however, didn't ask for an explanation. As I returned to my spot near the hearth, he placed the coiled wire before him on the desk and folded his hands again.

"The situation of which I speak may subject our family to a certain amount of public scrutiny," he said. "I wish to make it clear that I, and I alone, will speak for the family. I expect the rest of you to refer all queries to me."

Lord Elstyn cleared his throat and I sensed that he was about to come to the heart of the matter. I set my shoulder bag on the floor, surveyed the faces turned toward his, and saw nothing in them but rapt attention.

"Four months ago," he said, "Simon received the first of a series of anonymous, threatening messages, three of which he subsequently brought to me. . . ."

As the earl described the notes and the nature of the threats, Gina's increasingly angry frown told me that neither Simon nor Lord Elstyn had let her in on their secret.

"Due to a minor indisposition, I was unable to give the matter my full attention." The earl skipped over his heart attack as lightly as I would have skipped over a head cold. "While I was recovering, certain possibilities presented themselves to me. After some thought, I decided to enlist the help of a professional to investigate those possibilities."

He reached over to press a button on his desk. A moment later Jim Huang entered the study, carrying his laptop computer and the manuscript box. The young archivist had pulled a navy-blue V-neck sweater over his rumpled white shirt and combed his jet-black hair, but his almond eyes were as anxious as they'd been the first time I'd encountered him in the library.

He paused just inside the doorway, as if uncertain of his welcome, before moving swiftly to place the box and the computer on the desk. He opened both, fiddled with the laptop's keyboard, then stood back, as if awaiting further instructions.

"Mr. James Huang"—Lord Elstyn raised a hand to indicate the new arrival—"is the son of an American business associate. He also works for Interpol."

My jaw dropped. I simply couldn't, by any contortion of the imagination, picture the slender, timid, bespectacled young book-lover packing an automatic and rounding up drug lords for the International Criminal Police Organization. Without thinking, I blurted, "You're an *Interpol agent?*"

My open incredulity made Jim blush.

"I'm not a field agent," he explained hastily. "I'm in document analysis."

Lord Elstyn silenced me with an oppressive glance. "Mr. Huang is an *expert* in document analysis," he emphasized. "He also has access to a wide range of useful information networks. With his help, I have been able to identify the person responsible for Simon's anonymous messages." He sat back in his chair. "Mr. Huang?"

Jim nervously pushed his oversized glasses up his nose, but his voice was surprisingly steady when he said, "There's a ninety-nine percent probability that the anonymous threats were sent by one of Lord Elstyn's former employees."

No one said a word, but an ax would have bounced off the tension in the room. Simon gripped my shoulder and I found myself mouthing the name of the earl's ex-valet: *Chambers* . . .

"My research indicates," Jim went on, "that the threats came from Miss Charlotte Elizabeth Winfield, who was employed as—"

"Winnie?" Derek jumped to his feet. "Nonsense! Utter nonsense! How *dare* you suggest that my *nanny* could be responsible for—"

"It's more than a suggestion, sir." Jim must have been very sure of himself because he faced Derek's wrath without flinching. "If you'll return to your seat, I'll explain."

Derek gave his father a mutinous glare, but Emma, Peter, and Bill managed to coax him back into his chair, where he sat with folded arms and a face like thunder.

Simon and I exchanged bewildered glances. His hand moved from my shoulder to his trouser pocket and I knew we were thinking the same thought: How had Derek's former nanny gotten ahold of the earl's straight razor?

"If you would lay the groundwork, sir . . ." Jim Huang nodded to the earl and stepped back.

"If I could spare you, my boy . . ." Lord Elstyn's eyes teemed with conflicting emotions as he gazed at Derek—regret, frustration, and hope overlaid with great reluctance. Then he lowered his gaze to the coiled wire and his expression hardened. "But I cannot. I can no longer protect you from the truth."

"What truth?" Derek demanded impatiently. "What are you talking about?"

"Miss Winfield showed signs of mental instability while you were under her care," Lord Elstyn replied bluntly. "She invented grandiose tales about her past and shared them with the other servants. Giddings informed me of the situation, but I was . . . preoccupied . . . at the time . . . by other, pressing concerns."

He was in London, I told myself, watching his wife die inch by inch.

"Apart from that," Lord Elstyn added in a firmer tone of voice, "you had become deeply attached to Miss Winfield. Since the fabrications seemed relatively harmless, I could not bring myself to sever a tie that brought you so much happiness."

Derek opened his mouth to speak, but Emma shook her head, so he contented himself with a derisive snort. The earl chose to overlook his son's show of disrespect.

"Eventually," Lord Elstyn continued, "a report came to my ears that I could not ignore. Miss Winfield had taken up with my valet, a man called Chambers." The earl shrugged. "Such things happen, even in the best-regulated households, but when I learned"—he leaned forward and spoke directly to Derek—"when I learned that the pair of them had left you, Simon, and Oliver alone near the lake while they disported themselves in the shrubbery, I was compelled to take action." He looked pleadingly at his son. "You were seven years old, Derek. Oliver was a mere toddler. Anything might have happened."

"The fishing trips," Simon breathed.

"The day after you left for school," Lord Elstyn said, "
dismissed them both, Chambers as well as Miss Winfield
I didn't know at the time that Miss Winfield was preg
nant."

Derek became very still. "Winnie . . . pregnant?"

Jim Huang stepped forward, as if to support the earl'
claim. "Five months after Miss Winfield's departure, th
first of three groups of letters arrived at Hailesham Park
They were addressed to you, Mr. Harris, under your, er
original name: Anthony Elstyn."

"What letters?" Derek asked. "I never received any let
ters from Winnie."

"Lord Elstyn intercepted them," Jim said.

"They were full of lies," the earl put in. "She accuse
me of fathering her child and pleaded with you to inter
cede on her behalf—you, a *schoolboy*."

"Chambers had deserted her." Jim clasped his hand
behind his back and delivered his report with an air of clin
ical detachment that stood in stark contrast to the raw
emotions flowing between father and son. "His abandon
ment triggered the first spate of letters. Some were sen
directly to your prep school. . . ."

Other letters had been sent to Hailesham Park, but th
earl had intercepted all of them. After reading the firs
half-dozen, he instructed Giddings to place Winnie's let
ters in storage, unopened, whenever they arrived.

Jim placed his hand on the manuscript box. "Gidding
stored the documents in the butler's safe, along with th
family silver."

"I intended to give them to you one day, when yo
were old enough to understand what had happened,'

Lord Elstyn said, still speaking to his son. "But by the time you were old enough—"

"I'd left." Derek ran a hand through his unkempt salt-and-pepper curls. He stared at the floor for a moment, then looked at Jim Huang. "You mentioned other letters. What became of them?"

"Giddings continued to follow his instructions," Jim answered. "He filed the letters without consulting Lord Elstyn. It wasn't until the recent threats arrived that Lord Elstyn asked to see the storage boxes."

"Giddings brought ten boxes to me, filled with hundreds of unopened letters," said the earl. "I was appalled by the number that had accumulated over the years. There were far too many for me to deal with."

Jim consulted his computer screen. "Miss Winfield sent a total of seven hundred and twenty-three letters to you, Mr. Harris. The first thirty-five were sent shortly after Chambers's desertion. . . ."

Jim Huang had read every letter. At the same time, he'd reconstructed nearly forty years of Winnie's life by following the postal codes on her envelopes. Once he'd determined her location, he'd utilized his computer skills to search the records of various social-service agencies for more detailed information. The paper trail he'd followed was strewn with heartache.

"Miss Winfield never blamed you for failing to answer her letters," said Jim. "She assumed that your father had forbidden you to have any contact with her."

"Yet she kept writing," Derek murmured. He seemed dazed.

"She was not a well woman," Jim said. "She had a minor breakdown after Chambers left." He clicked a key on the computer. "She was treated for depression at a clinic in Manchester. It was while she was undergoing treatment that she began writing to you. . . ."

Motherhood seemed to have a stabilizing effect on Winnie. She wrote to Derek to tell him that she'd given birth to a healthy baby boy, whom she'd named Anthony. Thirteen years passed before she wrote again.

"You were about to come of age, Mr. Harris," Jim explained. "Miss Winfield scanned the society columns, searching for news of the celebrations surrounding your twenty-first birthday."

"There was no celebration," Derek said shortly.

"There was no mention of you at all," Jim pointed out. "There were, however, many references to your cousin, Simon Elstyn."

Simon groaned softly and covered his eyes with his hand.

"She grew suspicious of your cousin," Jim continued. "She wrote twenty times to warn you against"—he tapped his keyboard and bent to read aloud from the screen—"'Simon's sly plot to snatch Hailesham away from you.'"

"She was always suspicious of Simon," the earl added wearily. "She expressed mistrust of him in her earliest letters, accused him of currying favor with me, though he was a mere child. That's why she came to mind when Simon brought the anonymous notes to me."

"She was never entirely rational about Simon," Jim agreed. "She believed Simon had betrayed her and Chambers to Giddings."

"I didn't," Simon protested. "I didn't know they were . . ." He looked helplessly from Derek to Oliver. "I thought Chambers played with us because he liked us."

"As I said, sir, Miss Winfield wasn't entirely rational." Jim consulted his computer. "When she was twenty-five, she was diagnosed as manic-depressive. She was on medication for many years thereafter and seemed to be functioning fairly well. . . ."

Having done her duty by warning Derek, Winnie refocused her attention on her own life. She found work waitressing at a swanky restaurant in London, played the organ at her church, and raised her son. At eighteen, young Anthony joined the army. He became an electronics specialist. Winnie was extremely proud of him.

While Jim droned on about Anthony's spotless service record, my attention drifted to the coil of wire on Lord Elstyn's desk. I couldn't help wondering if the young electronics specialist had taught his mother how to rig radio-controlled devices, such as a set of flashbulbs that could be conveniently hidden in trailing ivy. My dark musings were interrupted by a subtle change in Jim Huang's tone. His clipped, businesslike delivery slowed, and when I looked up, I saw a shadow of regret cross his face.

"Four years later, at the age of twenty-two," he said, "while on training maneuvers in the Lake District, Anthony Chambers died."

A collective sigh wafted through the study. Even Gina seemed moved by Winnie's loss.

Jim touched a finger to his glasses. "He was killed while demonstrating a new device for disarming land mines. The device failed. The mine exploded. His death is a matter of public record. . . ."

After the funeral Winnie had a major breakdown. She was hospitalized for a year. When she was released, she began writing again.

"From then on she wrote once, sometimes twice a week," said Jim. "There's a marked deterioration in her handwriting during this period, and the postal codes vary more often, as she moved from place to place. She began to draw heavily on memories of her days at Hailesham Park. One letter in particular is worth noting. . . ."

Winnie had seen a magazine article describing the restoration of a twelfth-century church in Shropshire. The article had caught her eye because the man in charge of the project had a familiar name.

When she'd seen the accompanying photograph, her troubled mind had begun to race. Why did the photograph identify Anthony Evelyn Armstrong Seton, Viscount Hailesham, as Derek Harris? Why was Lord Hailesham in Shropshire, restoring an old church, when he should have been at his father's side, managing the family estate? What had happened to her beloved boy?

Her interest in Derek became an obsession.

"She visited Finch, the village near your home," said Jim. "She listened to village gossip but learned nothing. No one there seemed aware of your true identity. . . ."

Winnie then returned to Hailesham, ostensibly to view the gardens. While there, she called on old Mr. Harris, who told her about Derek's estrangement from his father. He also told her that Derek had a son of his own who would come of age in ten years' time.

"In a way, Miss Winfield's obsession helped her," Jim observed. "It gave her a purpose, a goal, a reason to get up every day and go on living."

"What was her goal?" Emma asked.

"She wanted to make sure that Peter's twenty-first birthday was celebrated properly," Jim replied. "She wanted Peter to have that which Derek had willingly given up—the title, the prestige, the wealth. She spelled out her plan explicitly in her letters. . . ."

Winnie began to reestablish her credentials in the service industry. She went to court and changed her last name to Chambers. She used the contacts she'd made while waitressing at the fancy London restaurant and started at the bottom, cleaning the houses of the restaurant's well-heeled customers. She accumulated references and worked her way up through the ranks. By the end of the decade, Charlotte Chambers was more than qualified to sign on with the agency Giddings patronized.

"When Giddings requested a respectable maid-of-all-work four months ago, she was ready." Jim closed his laptop. "I can't speak to her actions after she came to Hailesham."

"Let's hope Giddings can," said Lord Elstyn.

The earl touched the button on his desk and Giddings entered the study. The elderly manservant was accompanied by a dark-suited underling carrying a large cardboard box. The nameless assistant deposited the box on the desk, beside Jim Huang's computer, and stood back. Giddings took his place beside the earl's desk.

"Well?" said Lord Elstyn.

Giddings bowed. "Please allow me to offer my sincerest apologies, my lord. Had I been more alert, I might have—"

"Yes, all right Giddings," the earl barked, "get on with it."

Giddings straightened with alacrity. "We searched the servants' quarters, my lord, as you requested. I'm afraid we made some rather disturbing discoveries."

Lord Elstyn eyed the box suspiciously as Giddings drew from it a clear plastic bag containing a sheet of paper. The paper looked as if it had been crumpled, then smoothed flat.

"We found this document and many others like it in Miss . . . Winfield's room," said Giddings. "I believe, with regret, that she obtained the documents from your waste receptacle, my lord, in the course of her normal duties."

Lord Elstyn nodded grimly for Giddings to go on.

Giddings lifted a second plastic bag from the box. It seemed to contain a cloth cap. A third bag held what appeared to be a pair of rough trousers. A fourth held a moth-eaten woolen sweater.

"When I approached Miss Winfield's wardrobe," Giddings explained, "I detected a strong scent of paraffin, similar to the scent you noted on the night of the fire, my lord." He swept a hand over the bagged clothing. "These items of apparel were hidden well back in the wardrobe. I can only assume that Miss Winfield used them to disguise herself when she retrieved the paraffin from the greenhouse and used it to set the topiary ablaze."

Beside me, Simon stirred. He put his hand in his pocket, walked to the desk, and deposited the straight razor atop the pile of bagged clothing.

"It's one of your old cutthroats, Uncle," he said to the earl. "You must have given it to Chambers, who left it behind when he abandoned Winnie. I believe she left it in the nursery."

"The nursery?" Lord Elstyn queried.

"She cut up the children's books," Simon told him. "She used the books in the nursery to create her anonymous threats. You'll find paper and paste in the toy cupboard."

"Thank you, sir," said Giddings. "We shall look into it immediately."

Simon returned to my side. There was no trace of triumph in his demeanor. He looked self-conscious and ashamed, as if grieved by the knowledge that he could no longer plead innocent to Winnie's charge of betrayal.

"You did the right thing," I murmured. "If you hadn't told them, I would have."

"It's like kicking a child," he said sadly.

"A dangerous child," I reminded him.

Giddings lifted another clear plastic bag from the cardboard box. "I'm not entirely certain whether this item is relevant or not, my lord, but since it was bundled with the clothing, I thought it best to bring it along. It has antennae, my lord. It appears to be a control mechanism of some kind."

"I know what it is." Lord Elstyn lifted the coil of wire and let it drop, as though he couldn't bear to touch it. "It was used to control an evil device hidden in the ivy covering the hurdles. My granddaughter informed me this morning that Ms. Shepherd discovered the device last night."

Simon looked down at me. "When did you . . ."

"After I left you, it just came to me," I muttered, offering a reasonable approximation of the truth. "Your fall, Nell's—no accident."

"Miss Winfield tried to kill Simon twice, to prevent him from taking my son's place," Lord Elstyn was saying. "She used remote-controlled flashbulbs to spook Deacon. The second time, she mistook Eleanor for Simon."

"Dear Lord . . ." Simon gasped angrily and raised his voice to Giddings. "How could you allow her to come under our roof? Didn't you recognize her?"

"It has been almost forty years, sir, since I last encountered Miss Winfield," Giddings replied with unflappable aplomb. "Her appearance has altered greatly."

His words tweaked my memory and I began to see the light. "She put on weight," I said. "She dyed her hair red."

"Madam?" said Giddings with polite perplexity.

"She's masquerading as the red-haired maid." I pointed at Jim Huang. "Jim told us that Winnie played the organ at her church. I caught the red-haired maid playing the piano in the drawing room yesterday. She must be—"

"I don't believe it," Derek declared. He stared stubbornly at his father. "Winnie might have threatened Simon. She might even have burnt the turtledove in some misguided effort to help me. But *attempted murder*? Never. Not Winnie. She couldn't do such a thing."

"I knew you would resist the idea," said Lord Elstyn. "I'd hoped to avoid a direct confrontation, but . . ." He reached for the button on his desk.

Twenty-two

Giddings scooped up the bagged items and dropped them into the box, which his assistant whisked out of sight behind the desk. The elderly manservant then straightened his tie and went to stand at the door.

The door opened. The red-haired maid entered, carrying the tea tray. She curtsied.

"More tea, sir?" she asked.

"No, thank you," said Giddings, and took the tray from her.

The maid glanced up at his forbidding scowl. Her eyes darted from face to face around the room. When they met Derek's, he half rose from his chair.

"Winnie?" he said.

She took her bottom lip between her teeth and lowered her lashes. When she looked up again, her face was wreathed in the sweetest of smiles.

"Now, Master Anthony, what did I tell you about standing when a servant comes into the room?" she chided.

She smoothed her apron and approached Derek, who'd sunk back into his chair. He was so tall and she so tiny that when she stood before him, they were nearly eye to eye.

"Didn't I tell you to stand only for ladies?" she asked.

"Polite indifference, that's what you show to servants, remember?"

"Yes, Winnie," said Derek.

"I knew you'd come back to help your son. I had a son, too, but . . ." Her face went slack for a moment and her eyes became hollow caves. Then the sweet smile returned, the adoring animation. "Did you enjoy your treacle tart, my pet? I made it for you, right under Cook's nose—the porridge, too—and she never tumbled." Her smile widened. "Who's the clever boots?"

"You are, Winnie," Derek replied as if the exchange was a familiar one, fond words spoken in childhood and never forgotten.

"My, my," she crooned. "Haven't you grown to be a fine, strong, handsome man?" She plucked playfully at Derek's curls. "Your hair needs trimming, there's no denying, and those boots . . ." She clucked her tongue. "Haven't brushed them in a month, I'll wager. Naughty. I had to dust the nursery all over again after you visited Blackie."

"Sorry, Winnie."

"I'm sorry, too," she said, cupping his face in her wrinkled hands, "dreadfully sorry about your precious little girl. I never meant to harm her, but you know that, don't you, my pet?"

"I know, Winnie."

"It was meant for *him*." As she glanced at Simon, Winnie's face writhed into a venomous mask that vanished instantly when she turned back to Derek. "I tried to warn him, but he wouldn't listen. Won't listen must be made to listen." She leaned close to Derek's ear and hissed in an audible whisper: *"Make him drink his tea. . . ."*

No one spoke. No one moved. Derek closed his eyes.

"There, now, Master Anthony." Winnie straightened. "Speak up for your son when the time comes. Don't let them bully you."

"I won't." Derek swallowed hard.

Giddings rattled the tea tray peremptorily. "Come along, Miss Winfield. Master Anthony must attend to his affairs."

"Yes, Mr. Giddings. Sorry, Mr. Giddings." Winnie gave Derek's hair a last motherly caress. "Good-bye, my pet."

"Good-bye . . . Winnie." The muscles worked in Derek's jaw as he watched his beloved nanny meekly take the tea tray from Giddings and leave.

The others shrank back as Winnie passed them, as if her madness were a contagion that might be spread by contact. I turned and stared in horror at the teacup sitting on the mantelshelf.

"Inspector Layton?" Lord Elstyn murmured.

Giddings's dark-suited assistant stepped forward, but he did so with an air of authority that had been missing when he'd first entered the study.

"My men are waiting for her, Lord Elstyn," he said. "I've instructed them to treat her with care. Huang has already made his report. I'll send a chap round to take statements from everyone else this afternoon." He picked up the cardboard box and addressed the rest of us. "In the meantime, please don't touch the teacup intended for Simon Elstyn. We'll want to analyze its contents. Good day to you all."

Giddings opened the door for Inspector Layton and gave him a deferential bow as he passed. Jim Huang retrieved his laptop and was about to follow the inspector out of the study when the earl asked him to wait.

"Thank you, Mr. Huang," he said.

"You're welcome, sir," said Jim.

"I would be honored," the earl continued, "if you would accept a volume from the library, any volume you choose, as a special token of my family's gratitude."

"Any volume?" Jim echoed, wide-eyed. He seemed to doubt his good fortune. "As I'm sure you know, sir, some of the books are quite valuable."

"None can be as valuable as the service you've rendered us," said the earl. "Go, Mr. Huang, make your selection. You are a connoisseur. I know that you will give it a good home. And please give my best regards to your father."

"I will, sir. Thank you, sir." Jim bounced on his toes as he departed, as if he couldn't wait to reach the library.

When Giddings had gone, Bill and I were the only non–family members left in the study, but I didn't think it mattered. After the morning's wrenching revelations, I doubted that anyone would have the heart to discuss business. I should have known better.

"Yes," Gina said, flicking the file folder with her fingertip. "We've been subjected to a most disagreeable scene, but now that it's over, we should take a page from Giddings's book and attend to our affairs."

"Surely it can wait," pleaded Oliver.

"It has waited," Gina retorted. "It's waited for more than twenty years. Uncle and I have spent the past three months preparing for this meeting and I'm damned if I'll have it delayed another second." She snapped her fingers, as if she'd had a sudden insight. "The papers Winfield dug out of the rubbish," she said. "She must have found your notes, Uncle. She must have read the outline of my plan—"

"A plan to which I am adamantly opposed," Bill interrupted.

Gina sniffed. "Bill's been your staunch defender, Derek. I'm surprised he has any voice left, after arguing so forcibly on your behalf, but Uncle's mind is made up."

Simon stepped into the fray. "Will someone please tell me what's going on?"

"Don't be naive, Simon," Claudia drawled. "Even I've been able to guess that Uncle Edwin intends to disinherit Derek."

"What?" Simon looked thunderstruck. "Don't be absurd, Claudia. Uncle Edwin would never disinherit his own son."

Derek swung around to face him. The heartache he felt for Winnie erupted in a blast of anger directed at his cousin. "Stop pretending, Simon. Winnie was right. You've been angling for my position ever since we were children."

Oliver tried to intervene. "Derek, I don't think you understand—"

"I understand everything," Derek broke in. "The moment my back was turned, Simon was there. 'Watch me ride, Uncle Edwin, watch me dance. Read my school reports, introduce me to your friends, *choose my wife for me. . . .*' Your ambition would be laughable if it weren't so disgusting."

I would have fled from Derek's taunting, but Simon held his ground.

"If I was there, Derek, it was *because* your back was

turned," he said. "Someone had to help Uncle Edwin. Someone had to be there for him after Aunt Eleanor died, and *you weren't*."

Derek rose to his feet, fists clenched. "Don't you dare bring my mother into this."

"Your mother's at the very center of it," Simon retorted. "If you hadn't spent so much time trailing after the carpenter, you'd know—"

"Now you're going to insult Mr. Harris?" Derek's voice rose in disbelief. "Mr. Harris was a better husband than my father ever was. Mr. Harris's wife never left him."

I stared at Derek, aghast, knowing he'd spoken in ignorance and wishing I could hold back the avalanche of harsh truth that was about to hit him. But there was no holding it back.

"Your mother didn't leave your father." Simon bit off each word and spat it out angrily. "She died, Derek. She died of cancer. She took a year to die, and when she was done, your father would have turned to you, but you'd already shut him out." Simon paused to catch his breath. "So he turned to me. I've spent my entire life making up for your shortcomings and I've paid for it, oh, how I've paid."

Gina stood. "You're about to be repaid, Simon. Uncle Edwin, would you please make your announcement?"

The earl didn't seem to hear her. He was staring at Derek as if mesmerized. "Anthony," he said softly, "have you believed, for all these years, that your mother abandoned you?"

"She . . . she left me because of you," Derek faltered.

"No, my boy, no." Lord Elstyn pushed himself up from his chair and came to stand before Derek. "She wanted to protect you. She didn't want you to see her suffer. She wouldn't allow me to bring you to her." The earl seemed to shrink beneath the weight of memory, and his voice sank to a broken murmur, but his eyes remained fixed on Derek's. "She lost her hair, her fingernails, her teeth. Her skin turned gray, her body shriveled. You were her darling child, the only child she would ever have. She didn't want you to remember her that way. She wouldn't let me tell you. . . ." The earl shook his head. "I meant to explain when you were older, but time slipped away. You were at school, at university—and then you were gone."

Derek looked heartsick and confused. His voice trembled as he said, "Father?"

Lord Elstyn put a hand on his son's shoulder, whispering, "My boy . . ."

If I could have pulled out a magic wand and made everyone but those two disappear, I would have. The moment was sacred. It belonged to one father and one son, and no one else should have been there to witness it.

Bill was on the same wavelength. He rose quietly and motioned for the others to follow him out of the study. They would have, if Gina hadn't raised her voice.

"No," she said, then repeated more determinedly, "*No.* It's too late for reconciliation. The papers are signed. Simon will assume control of Hailesham's assets upon Uncle Edwin's decease."

"No, he will not," Simon growled.

"Don't meddle," Gina snapped. "You don't know how hard I've worked to make this happen."

"It's a pity you didn't discuss it with me," said Simon. Gina flung the file folder on the desk in exasperation.

"Why are you being so obstructive? You love Hailesham. I know you do. It's what you've always wanted."

All eyes turned to Simon. He gazed across the room at his wife, staring at her as if she were a stranger. Finally he smiled.

"You're right," he conceded. "I do love Hailesham." He put his hands in his trouser pockets, strolled slowly to the windows, and let his gaze rove from the workshops to the stables. He inhaled deeply. "I love the house, the woods, the gardens, but, above all, I love the tradition. It's a tradition that goes back some eight hundred years—for eight centuries the land's been handed down from father to son, without interruption." He looked over his shoulder at his wife. "Did you seriously believe that I, of all people, would be the one to break the chain?"

Gina's look of blazing hatred seemed to scorch the air. "If you refuse," she said, "you're on your own."

Simon shrugged. "I've been on my own for years." He turned his face to the windows. "It won't hurt to make it official."

Gina reached for the folder, but Claudia darted forward and snatched it from the desk. "Yours, I think, Uncle Edwin," she said. "Your papers. Your decision."

Lord Elstyn turned to Gina, saying, "I'm sorry."

"You will be," she said evenly, and marched out of the study.

A moment of silence followed her departure. Then Lord Elstyn laid the folder on the desk, opened it, and began tearing up the closely written sheets of paper it contained.

Derek put a hand out to stop him. "Father," he said hesitantly, "you know I can't come back. I can't be Anthony again. I have my own life and it's a good one."

"You have a son," Lord Elstyn pointed out. "In two short weeks, he'll come of age."

I felt a rush of trepidation for Peter. He was at home sailing the high seas, paddling dugout canoes, manning vulcanologists' outposts. He was too young to trade the carefree adventures of the open road for the heavy responsibilities of family leadership.

Peter folded his hands in his lap and tapped the tips of his thumbs together. His gaze was focused inward, as if he were contemplating the diverging paths that stretched before him. He seemed to reach a decision. He stood, sauntered past his father and grandfather, and came to a halt at Simon's side. Both men gazed out at the courtyard.

"Heard you might be in need of new digs," Peter said conversationally.

"I doubt that Gina will let me back into the old one," Simon observed.

"Don't suppose you'd care to live here," said Peter.

Simon took a shaky breath and bowed his head.

"On a permanent basis, I mean," Peter clarified. "I've got a few commitments to keep over the next couple of years. It'd be comforting to know that Grandfather has someone—someone close at hand—on whom he can rely absolutely while I'm away."

Simon opened his mouth to speak, but the words seemed to catch in his throat.

"I'll need to learn the ropes when I come back, of course," Peter went on. "Should take years and years. The rest of my life, in fact. I'm rather counting on you being here to teach me." His steady gaze came to rest on Simon's face. "I've always counted on you to be here."

"I . . ." Simon struggled for composure. "I'll do my best, Peter. I swear to you, I'll do my best."

"Right. Good. Well, that's settled then." Peter's hand rested lightly on Simon's shoulder, then he turned to address the others. "I promised Nell I'd tell her what happened here this morning, but so much has happened that I'm not sure I can do it on my own. Would anyone care to lend a hand?"

"We'll all come," said Emma, and everyone murmured their assent.

"Excellent." Peter strode forward, gathering his shaken family as he went. "Though my promise strikes me now as a bit ridiculous. Knowing my sister as I do, I've little doubt that she'll end up telling *us* what happened."

His comment provoked a muted ripple of laughter. Peter seemed to know that old wounds healed best when given a judicious dose of sunshine.

Derek waited until the others had gone, then turned to gaze at Simon, who remained standing at the windows.

"Simon," he said softly, "where do I begin . . ."

Simon drew a breath and let it out slowly. "Use your skills," he said. "Start rebuilding some old bridges."

Derek nodded gravely, turned, and left the room.

I stayed behind with Simon.

"You okay?" I asked.

"I'm not sure," he answered, "but apart from my ribs, which are still rather tender, I believe that I may be better than I've been in ages." He took his hands from his pockets and held them out to me. "You said something—was it only yesterday? You said that a life without risk isn't worth living. Perhaps I've taken my first step toward rebirth."

"Sounds painful." I took his hands in mine and held them tightly. "If you need any help along the way . . ."

"I'll ask for help"—he pressed my hands to his heart—"from my friend."

Epilogue

S imon collected a few personal items from his home, then moved into a suite of rooms at Hailesham Park. Though his son is a regular visitor, his soon-to-be-ex-wife is not. Lord Elstyn has already found a new attorney.

Lord Elstyn has found a new hobby as well. Emma coaxed him into the greenhouses one wintry day and persuaded him—no one knows how—to repot a geranium. He's taken a hands-on approach to gardening ever since, and it seems to have given him a new lease on life. When the tourists come in the spring and see a tall and stately gentleman wheeling barrows of compost down the paths, they'll find it hard to believe that he ever had a heart problem.

The problems besetting Derek's heart are more complex and will take longer to work out. He's trying hard to forge a new relationship with Simon as well as his father, and with goodwill on all sides, I'm confident he'll succeed.

The doctors have asked Derek not to visit Winnie. She was deemed incompetent to stand trial and confined to a secure nursing home, where she coddles the cat and keeps her room—and everyone else's—immaculate. I don't think she'll ever be released.

Claudia will never become a doctor, but she's put her social standing to good use by holding fund-raisers to support a cancer hospice. Her husband the MP cites her accomplishments with pride in his news releases, and the Westwood Trust now counts her as one of its most active and dependable patrons.

Oliver took me up on my invitation to visit the cottage. He spent Thanksgiving weekend helping Annelise chase after the boys while I basted the turkey, and he returned a week later, to bring Annelise a book she'd mentioned in passing. Since he's not the kind of man to rush a courtship, I figure I'll have until St. Patrick's Day to find another nanny.

Peter returned to New Zealand to finish his whale survey, but Emma tells me that his next project will take him no farther than the Shetland Islands, where he'll spend the summer counting seals—and keeping his finger on the family pulse.

After two weeks of recuperation at Hailesham, Nell went back to Paris. When she failed to materialize at Christmas, Kit gave the boys rides in Rosie's sleigh, and young Rainey Dawson, a neighbor's granddaughter, won the coveted role of the Virgin in the nativity play. We're all hoping the Honorable Nell will come home at Easter, on the arm of Pierre or Jean-Luc or François.

On the whole, Dimity enjoyed her visit to Hailesham Park. She was particularly proud of me for resisting the obvious temptations. When I admitted that it had been touch-and-go for about a millisecond, she asked what had held me back.

I smiled as the answer came to me, ready-made. "Why would I settle for a noble heart, bags of charm, and a pair of beguiling dimples when I have all of that and so much more with Bill?"

My answer seemed to satisfy Aunt Dimity, though I haven't heard from her in a while. When we last spoke, she told me she'd need at least a month to recover from our five-day holiday.

Winnie's Treacle Tart

1 9-inch pie shell

FILLING

1½ cups light corn syrup combined with 1 teaspoon
    molasses
1½ cups fresh soft white bread crumbs
1 tablespoon fresh lemon juice
½ teaspoon ground ginger
1 egg, lightly beaten

Prepare, but do not bake, your favorite pie shell.

Preheat the oven to 350 degrees Fahrenheit.

In a large bowl, combine the corn syrup–molasses mixture, bread crumbs, lemon juice, ginger, and egg. Stir until the ingredients are well combined. Pour the mixture into the pie shell, smoothing it out with a spatula. The shell should be about two-thirds full.

Bake in the middle of the oven for 20 minutes, or until the filling is firm to the touch and the crust golden brown.

Cut the tart into wedges and serve at once.

FOR THE BEST IN PAPERBACKS, LOOK FOR THE

In every corner of the world, on every subject under the sun, Penguin represents quality and variety—the very best in publishing today.

For complete information about books available from Penguin—including Penguin Classics, Penguin Compass, and Puffins—and how to order them, write to us at the appropriate address below. Please note that for copyright reasons the selection of books varies from country to country.

In the United States: Please write to *Penguin Group (USA), P.O. Box 12289 Dept. B, Newark, New Jersey 07101-5289* or call 1-800-788-6262.

In the United Kingdom: Please write to *Dept. EP, Penguin Books Ltd, Bath Road, Harmondsworth, West Drayton, Middlesex UB7 0DA.*

In Canada: Please write to *Penguin Books Canada Ltd, 10 Alcorn Avenue, Suite 300, Toronto, Ontario M4V 3B2.*

In Australia: Please write to *Penguin Books Australia Ltd, P.O. Box 257, Ringwood, Victoria 3134.*

In New Zealand: Please write to *Penguin Books (NZ) Ltd, Private Bag 102902, North Shore Mail Centre, Auckland 10.*

In India: Please write to *Penguin Books India Pvt Ltd, 11 Panchsheel Shopping Centre, Panchsheel Park, New Delhi 110 017.*

In the Netherlands: Please write to *Penguin Books Netherlands bv, Postbus 3507, NL-1001 AH Amsterdam.*

In Germany: Please write to *Penguin Books Deutschland GmbH, Metzlerstrasse 26, 60594 Frankfurt am Main.*

In Spain: Please write to *Penguin Books S. A., Bravo Murillo 19, 1° B, 28015 Madrid.*

In Italy: Please write to *Penguin Italia s.r.l., Via Benedetto Croce 2, 20094 Corsico, Milano.*

In France: Please write to *Penguin France, Le Carré Wilson, 62 rue Benjamin Baillaud, 31500 Toulouse.*

In Japan: Please write to *Penguin Books Japan Ltd, Kaneko Building, 2-3-25 Koraku, Bunkyo-Ku, Tokyo 112.*

In South Africa: Please write to *Penguin Books South Africa (Pty) Ltd, Private Bag X14, Parkview, 2122 Johannesburg.*